Arrogant Beggar

Anzia Yezierska

Arrogant Beggar

Introduction by Katherine Stubbs

Duke University Press Durham and London 1996

First published in 1927 by Doubleday, Page & Co.

© 1927, 1954 Louise Levitas Henriksen

This edition and Introduction © 1996 Duke University Press

All rights reserved

Printed in the United States of America on acid-free paper ∞

Library of Congress Cataloging-in-Publication Data

appear on the last printed page of this book.

Second printing, 1997

Contents

Introduction by Katherine Stubbs

When *Arrogant Beggar* was published in 1927, genteel critics reacted with uneasy disdain. The *New York Tribune* accused Anzia Yezierska of displaying "a complete and amusing ignorance of gentile minds, and somehow a faint lack of good taste." The reviewer for the *New York World* confessed to feeling "cold" toward Yezierska's "unpleasant" style, her "high-handed impatience at the existing order of things." Their alarm was justified. *Arrogant Beggar* is a novel designed to dismantle a hallowed institution of American philanthropy. It offers a scathing critique of charity-run boarding houses for working women, an exposé of "the whole sickening farce of Big Sistering the Working Girl."

In writing this devastating indictment, Yezierska was expressing a rage born of personal experience. Years earlier, she had lived at the Clara de Hirsch Home for working women; during the same period, her education had been financially sponsored by a wealthy patron, Mrs. Ollesheimer. While there is little doubt that Yezierska's encounters with these forms of charity provided the narrative material and emotional impetus for her novel, the bitter disillusionment and moral outrage that form the first section of *Arrogant Beggar* may well have had an additional source. By 1927, Yezierska had come to realize that her literary reputation had dramatically declined. The writer whose life had once been legendary now found herself increasingly thrust from the spotlight.

At the height of Yezierska's success in the early 1920s, this legend had been as famous as her writing. The "sweatshop Cinderella" account of her life, printed in various forms in dozens of newspapers, went something like this. She was born into poverty in the Russian-Polish village of Plotsk, sometime around the year 1880 (perhaps due to a shtetl superstition regarding birthdays, Yezierska's exact birthday was never recorded). When Yezierska was about ten, she and her large family fled the czar's pogroms, sailing in steerage to the promised land, America. But the family's new life in the Jewish ghetto of New York's Lower East Side was one of terrible privation. Her father was a Hebrew scholar, and in accordance with Old World tradition, he expected to be economically supported by others so that he could devote himself to religious study. Because he refused to sully himself by earning money, he allowed Anzia to attend school only briefly before making her earn her keep. Yezierska (who had been given the Anglicized name Hattie Mayer) became at various times a servant, a scrub woman, and a factory worker. Writing in her scant spare time, with little knowledge of the English language, she sought to give voice to her fellow ghetto dwellers—to testify to their pain and to protest the inequities of the American economic system. Finally, after a struggle to write in the midst of overwhelming hardships, her tale "The Fat of the Land" was named the best short story of 1919. A year later, Houghton Mifflin published a collection of her stories under the title *Hungry Hearts* (Yezierska dedicated the collection to her former patron, Mrs. Ollesheimer—although there is evidence that she did so unwillingly). But despite the distinction of being a published writer, Yezierska remained on the edge of poverty until

Samuel Goldwyn paid her $10,000 for the film rights to her book. She then moved to California where she was soon living a life of glamour, welcomed into the ranks of glittering celebrity. It was a swift and dramatic ascent, a meteoric rise from Hester Street to Hollywood, from the sweatshop to fame and fortune. Thus went the legend, the public version of Anzia Yezierska's life.

Yet this legend is, necessarily, only partial—a series of omissions and half-truths. It omits, for instance, the entire period of Yezierska's life from about 1901 through 1919, when she could hardly be classified as an uneducated sweatshop worker. After earning a degree in domestic science from Columbia University Teachers College in 1904, Yezierska worked intermittently as a teacher. She briefly attended the American Academy of Dramatic Arts on a scholarship, and lived at the socialist Rand School. And although the legend tended to portray Yezierska as a young, single woman—alone and lonely in her poverty—she had in fact been married twice, first to an attorney in 1910 (the marriage was annulled) and then again in 1912 (to prevent the second marriage from being legally binding, she chose to have a religious ceremony only). Before separating from her second husband, she gave birth to a daughter. In 1917 and 1918, she had been professionally and personally associated with the famous philosopher John Dewey—a highly charged relationship which would form the subject matter of much of her fiction.

The drama of the "sweatshop Cinderella" version of Yezierska's life is generated by its selectivity; it is a study in contrasts, conforming to the conventions of a rags-to-riches narrative. But the legend effaces more than the facts of Yezierska's life. It also erases Yezierska's role as the creator of her own persona. For it is important to note that Yezierska's ability to mythologize herself contributed to her popular success in the early 1920s. Yezierska first came to Goldwyn's attention because the Hearst columnist Frank Crane wrote an article describing how Yezierska, "with comparatively little education, with no advantages, in a very hail of discouragements . . . produced stories . . . that put her at once in the front rank of American authors." Crane's article was a paean to Yezierska's genius—and he wrote it solely because Yezierska had entered his office, unannounced, and insisted upon describing herself to him. Crane explained to his readers, "She told her story, told it well, in a way to rejoice the heart of a newspaper person, in a few swift words, of keen beauty, redolent with individuality." Like the tale she spun in Crane's office, the stories Yezierska told about her life were persuasive; for a time, they sold, and the selling of her life story in newspaper articles, in Hollywood, seemed also to sell her fiction. The legend certainly helped to fuel the great publicity machine. In a public relations ploy for the sale of *Hungry Hearts,* Yezierska was given a lavish reception at the Waldorf-Astoria; the reception capitalized on a version of the Yezierska legend that depicted her as having once been turned away by the hotel when she applied for employment as a scullery maid.

Recognizing Yezierska's skill at self-promotion also necessitates acknowledging her deep ambivalence about the need for such promotion, her gradual disillusionment with the economic contingencies of artistic production. In *Red Ribbon on a White Horse: My Story,* published when Yezierska was nearly seventy, she described the dismay she experienced during her brief sojourn in Hollywood in 1921. The fierce commercialism of the motion picture industry shocked her and she objected to the way Goldwyn Pictures altered *Hungry Hearts* for commercial considerations. She soon discovered that Hollywood was nothing more than a "fish-market in evening clothes," where aesthetic considerations would always yield to the bottom line. Disgusted by Hollywood's "whirling race toward the spotlight, the frantic competition to outdistance the others, the machinery of success," and finding herself unable to write under such conditions, Yezierska returned to New York City. She published three more works, *Salome of the Tenements* (1923; also made into a film), the story collection *Children of Loneliness* (1923), and *Bread Givers* (1925), before writing *Arrogant Beggar*. *Arrogant Beggar* was written during the last financially secure period of Yezierska's life. By the publication of *All I Could Never Be* (1932), her last novel, the legendary success had long been over.

Yezierska herself appeared to be partly responsible for her literary decline. By the late 1920s, she was experiencing severe writer's block. Her method of composition had always been time-consuming, a laborious system whereby she would rewrite a story numerous times from start to finish before declaring it done. In the early piece "Mostly About Myself," she worried, "I never know whether the thoughts I've discarded are not perhaps better than the thoughts I've kept. With all the physical anguish I put into my work, I am never sure of myself." But now her subject matter had apparently run dry. In *Red Ribbon,* looking back at this period, she attributed her difficulty to the way she had distanced herself from her material. She had advertised herself as the voice of the downtrodden, but she had come to realize that her own experience with poverty had given her a deep ambivalence toward the poor. "Once you knew what poor people suffered it kept gnawing at you. You'd been there yourself. You wanted to reach out and help. But if you did, you were afraid you might be dragged back into the abyss"; "all I could feel was disgust—revulsion—escape. Anywhere—only away." Recalling that "I had gone too far away from life, and I did not know how to get back," she witnessed her literary reputation fade. The irony of her situation did not escape her. Friends who had pursued her now avoided her, and yet the image of her success remained; "The legend of my Cinderella success lived on while destitution stared me in the face." In 1929, she briefly held the Zona Gale fellowship, living as a writer-in-residence at the University of Wisconsin. During the Depression, having lost most of her money in the stock market crash, she spent time in the WPA Federal Writers Project. For decades she continued to write, but she could not get published.

It was only with the 1950 publication of *Red Ribbon on a White Horse,* with an introduction by W. H. Auden, that Anzia Yezierska reemerged into the world of letters. The book, subtitled "My Story," was not an autobiography but rather a crafted, highly selective account of certain moments in her past; although not a best seller, it was critically well-received. From 1951 to 1961, Yezierska wrote more than fifty book reviews for the *New York Times,* and published a number of essays and stories depicting the problems of the elderly in America. She died in Ontario, California, 22 November 1970.

Perhaps the central, tragic paradox of Yezierska's life as a writer lies in the fact that the legend which had once served to publicize her work ultimately contributed to her downfall. In the popular imagination, she had become so closely identified with her material that when opinion about immigrants and the working class shifted, her work was left behind. In a changing historical context, her "high-handed impatience at the existing order of things" no longer met with a sympathetic audience. It was not until the 1970s and 1980s, when scholars began to critique the traditional literary canon's exclusion of writings by women, members of the working class, and people of color, that Yezierska's early work was finally rediscovered. Anzia Yezierska is now being read and studied for the very reasons she was once dismissed.

If Yezierska's internal conflicts over her work and her writer's block hastened the waning of her reputation in the late 1920s, there were also other, more complex factors behind the decline of her literary fortunes. One set of factors was related to her choice of material. There were historical developments during the period that, in retrospect, can be seen to have conditioned the way readers reacted to Yezierska's subject matter. The initial receptivity to her female-centered fiction in the early 1920s came at a time when the independent New Woman and the adventurous Jazz Age flapper had both become familiar stereotypes, at least in urban areas; in 1920, women had at long last gained the vote. Moreover, Yezierska's brand of ethnic fiction, her focus on the lives of immigrants, came after two decades of Progressivism's social reformist rhetoric, which encouraged the general public's interest in the problems of the burgeoning population of Eastern and Southern European immigrants (a population that had exploded since 1890). It is thus possible to see Yezierska's early popularity as related to a new receptivity both to women's issues and to the experiences of immigrants.

But during the same period there was another set of developments that indicated a rising tide of conservatism, a wave of hostility to those ethnic groups that failed to conform to America's vision of itself as Anglo-Saxon. World War I had appeared to validate a national spirit of nativism and provided impetus for the intense educational campaign known as "Americanization," designed to indoctrinate immigrants into American cultural standards. In 1919 and 1920, the Palmer raids began, as Woodrow Wilson's Attorney General A. Mitchell Palmer executed mass raids on immigrants whom he suspected of being radicals; most of the aliens were working-class and of Russian origin. Alleging that these immigrants opposed the United States government, Palmer ordered hundreds of arrests and deportations (Yezierska's close friend Rose Pastor Stokes was among those arrested). In 1921 and 1924, revised quota systems severely restricted the immigration of peoples not of Western or Northern European origin. In 1920, the anarchists Nicola Sacco and Bartolomeo Vanzetti were accused of murder and in 1927, they were executed; the case against them appeared to be motivated, in large part, by hatred against working-class immigrants. During the same period, the eugenics movement and the new rising of the Ku Klux Klan signalled a national atmosphere of virulent racism and intolerance for non–Anglo-Saxon peoples. In this light, critics' growing impatience with Yezierska's subject matter by the late 1920s begins to make more sense.

What is more, Yezierska was unflinching in her focus on the impoverished and the working class during a time when the poorest Americans were not faring well. In the 1920s, working conditions for the lowest classes continued to be exceedingly difficult. Throughout the first decades of the twentieth century, striking workers were treated with appalling brutality (as incidents such as the Ludlow Massacre of 1914 attest). Indeed, Progressivism itself can be interpreted as an essentially conservative response to Establishment anxieties about the threat of labor radicalism, the rise of socialism, and the growing power of groups such as the International Workers of the World. Progressivism introduced reformist adjustments of the status quo that failed to touch the basic inequalities of the capitalist system while seeking to pacify those elements of the American population—the working class and immigrants—that agitated for change.

In her fiction, Yezierska not only refused to accept the conditions to which working-class immigrants were subjected, she also refused to accept those strains of Progressivism that were thinly-disguised attempts to manage the threat of the "foreign" to the American body politic. Yezierska was particularly incensed by the pseudo-scientific approach to health and hygiene proposed by the Progressivist domestic science movement. Indeed, it was while earning her degree in domestic science that she became profoundly alienated by the middle-class ideology's condescension. In numerous stories, Yezierska demonstrated that domestic science's standards of household management and food consumption were forms of cultural imperialism when indiscriminately prescribed to immigrants. Such a critique is salient in *Arrogant Beggar,* where Adele Lindner's initial resistance to the charity-run boarding home's domestic science course can be interpreted both as a resistance to becoming a servant, and as a resistance to cooking and cleaning methods at odds with her ethnic heritage and class background. Adele's decision to serve Jewish foods to the ghetto community is a further rejection of domestic science's veiled agenda of Americanization.

In the light of these historical factors, it becomes possible to examine more closely the role the Yezierska legend played in her literary decline. It is conceivable that it had a negative impact in two ways. First, the media's saturation with the Yezierska legend, and Yezierska's popular success in the early 1920s, may well have contributed to a critical backlash in the mid- and late 1920s. In rejecting Yezierska on the basis of her popularity, critics would have been performing the classic response of the literary establishment to female authors. Second, the Yezierska legend had become so well known that there was (and still continues to be) a notorious confusion about the distinction between Yezierska's own life and her fiction. Critics familiar with the legend noted that her protagonists were invariably Jewish women from the New York ghetto; they then accused Yezierska of repeatedly telling her own story. In writing much of her fiction in the first person, Yezierska appeared to convict herself of such a charge. Early confessions such as "I am aware that there's a little too much I—I—I, too much of self-analysis and introspection in my writing" also seemed to confirm the critics.

It is undeniable that Yezierska used many of her own experiences as inspiration for her fiction. But to treat Yezierska's fiction as nothing more than autobiography means overlooking her skill as an artist, as a shaper of representation. Because many critics believed her to be writing as a spokeswoman for the Jewish immigrant community (a perception encouraged by Yezierska herself), they tended to assess her writing in terms of its faithfulness to real Jewish immigrant experiences. Thus when her work was praised, it was often because of its "realism." When her work was criticized, the target was the work's inaccuracy, its failure to be realistic—in short, its sentimentality.

For if Yezierska's decline in reputation was in part a function of her subject matter, this decline was also related to her writing style. From the beginning, critics had been troubled by the sentimental style of her prose, the melodrama of her plots. By the late 1920s, her style, once praised for being vital and alive, was increasingly seen as excessive, as needing greater restraint and control. Indeed, many Yezierska readers continue to express reservations about the "quality" of her work. Historically, it has been writings by women and those writers marginalized by virtue of ethnicity or class that have been most vulnerable to the critical epithet "sentimental." Because of a long literary and mass cultural tradition, romance and the conventions of sentimentalism have been highly available languages for women. The sentimental was a genre traditionally dominated by female writers and readers; for many women interested in writing, the sentimental therefore provided a literary model. But for critics of early twentieth century literature, sentimentalism has traditionally been considered conventional—manipulative, simplistic, excessive—in contrast to modernism's formalist innovations and its interest in discontinuity and self-conscious experimentation. Against modernism's elitist position as high culture, sentimental discourse has traditionally been relegated to the popular. Implicit in these oppositions is an insidious gendering of the two traditions, as modernist discourses are coded as masculine, and the sentimental is feminized. Critics counterpose modernism's virile avant-garde stance against sentimentalism's unmediated transmission of a degraded mass culture (itself coded as female). Modernism was thus "modern" insofar as it depicted itself as heroically breaking with the depleted, effeminate, and genteel conventions of the nineteenth century; it thus defined itself, repeatedly, *against* the sentimental and all that the despised genre was thought to signify.

Just as feminist critics have recuperated the female-authored texts ignored by the traditional canon, critics such as Jane Tompkins and Suzanne Clark have begun interrogating traditional assumptions about the sentimental as a genre and as a narrative style. This means challenging the reflexive assumption that a text that is sentimental is of poor literary quality. It means that a sentimental style must be considered as a purposeful narrative strategy, a style capable of being mobilized for a variety of agendas. While its examination of gender and class may passively reinscribe the worst tendencies of patriarchal and capitalist ideologies, the sentimental can also be transgressive. Above all, because the sentimental was an idiom accessible to women, it must be recognized as a form that could be easily manipulated by female writers writing for their own ends.

When we go beyond modernist standards of literary assessment, we can consider Yezierska's writing style as a choice, a way of persuasively presenting the social and economic conditions of her narrative in a way that at moments strategically disregarded the contingencies of the realist formula. It is only when we take this style seriously that it becomes possible to see the way the sentimental was a mark of the Yiddish artistic tradition, a tradition of which Yezierska was acutely aware. A melodramatic style and overwrought emotionalism were prominent features of the Yiddish plays and literature that were popular on the Lower East Side during Yezierska's youth. Furthermore, when we consider the moralizing tone of texts such as *Arrogant Beggar,* Yezierska's use of a sentimental style appears all the more skillful; sentimental fiction has historically been used to persuade and has been uniquely well-suited to conveying ethical messages. Although "sophisticated" readers conditioned to expect complexity and ambiguity may have sneered at sentimental texts, the intellectual and psychological accessibility of these novels meant that they were capable of mobilizing a large number of readers on whom more subtle messages may have been lost. For many writers engaged in social criticism, the sentimental thus offered a valuable means of going beyond modernism's abstraction and relativism, its tendency to evade real-world political commitments.

Yezierska's choice of style is perhaps also partially responsible for another feature of her fiction that has attracted vigorous criticism. One characteristic of sentimental fiction is its reliance on stereotypes. As Jane Tompkins has noted, sentimental fiction frequently employs stereotypes as a form of shorthand, a way of condensing a large amount of cultural information for the reader. But Jewish critics found Yezierska's use of ethnic stereotypes to be deeply disturbing. By the late 1920s, early Jewish champions of her work had concluded that she parodied the incorrect English of immigrants and used unflattering stereotypes in her depictions of Jewish characters.

Of all the negative reactions of Yezierska's critics in the 1920s, the charge of racism has remained one of the most compelling critiques of her work. Throughout her fiction, Yezierska was concerned to represent the ethnic specificity of the speech and behavior of Jewish characters. But in practice, Yezierska's conception of Russian Jewish "racial traits" seemed to confirm pernicious clichés. Russian Jews consistently appear in her writing as excessively demonstrative, volatile, passionate and impulsive, emotionally hungry. In an even more damaging set of stereotypes, other Jewish characters are depicted as money-crazed, "fat-bellied" and avaricious sweatshop bosses, landlords, pawnbrokers, and merchants. These two ethnic stereotypes are often placed in narrative tension, as the female protagonist of a story is made to choose between a dreamy Jewish artist and a materialistic Jewish businessman. In contrast, assimilated "Anglo-Saxons" are stereotyped as emotionally remote, restrained, and rational. Such figures in Yezierska's fiction are usually male, and resemble Yezierska's descriptions of her real-life idol, John Dewey. These cultured, well-educated "higher-up" men recur throughout her work, where they seem to offer the promise of teaching the Russian Jewish female protagonist how to be "cold in the heart and clear in the head." The protagonist, in turn, offers such men spontaneity, eagerness for life. And in each situation—in texts such as "Wings," "The Miracle," "To the Stars," *Salome of the Tenements, All I Could Never Be*—there is a profound attraction, at times a "devouring affinity," between these representatives of what Yezierska saw as separate "races."

Jewish critics' anxieties about these stereotypes were well-founded. Although Yezierska's opposing characterization of the cold-blooded, cultured Anglo-Saxon and the hot-blooded, primitive "oriental" served her romantic plot, they also dangerously reinforced tenets of eugenicist theory that had gained a measure of intellectual prestige and popular support since the turn of the century. There is a little doubt that such stereotypes were yet another factor in Yezierska's decreased popularity. These portrayals, combined with Yezierska's focus on the dirt and poverty of the Jewish ghetto, may well have alienated those Jews who could have formed a section of her reading audience. Still close to their immigrant origins, they were perhaps anxious to have America overlook their ethnicity and the circumstances of their early lives. (Indeed, Yezierska's early popularity coincided with the highest population density of the Jewish Lower East Side; by the late 1920s, much of this population had migrated away from the ghetto to the outer boroughs of New York City, particularly Brooklyn and the Bronx.)

In reclaiming Anzia Yezierska from her early critics, it is not enough to understand why she was once dismissed. It is also crucial to appreciate the tradition in which she was writing, and to which she made unique contributions. There were certainly other Jewish Americans during this period who wrote about Jewish experiences; Yezierska shared many of the concerns of the writers who preceded her. She was aware of the success of Rose Cohen's 1918 autobiography, *Out of the Shadow*. Cohen was a Russian Jewish immigrant whose account of her early life strikingly paralleled Yezierska's own experiences. In her autobiography, Cohen outlined many of the themes that Yezierska would later explore, particularly the longing for education and independence. (Indeed, Yezierska would go on to write a story, "Wild Winter Love," directly based on Cohen's unhappy life.) Like Abraham Cahan in his 1917 novel, *The Rise of David Levinsky,* Yezierska was at times troubled by the paradox of worldly success; in much of her work, she explores the emptiness of wealth and fame, the way assimilation distances the immigrant from her roots and from herself. Yezierska also set forth themes that would continue to be the concern of later writers; as did Henry Roth in *Call It Sleep* and Michael Gold in *Jews Without Money,* Yezierska demonstrated the dark side of the Jewish immigrant experience in America, interrogating any tendency to assume that Jews enjoyed instant financial prosperity.

But Yezierska's work is most frequently lauded today for its groundbreaking focus on Jewish women and the dilemmas they faced. The assertive female protagonist of Yezierska's fiction is typically on a quest for education and self-realization, longing, in Yezierska's memorable phrase, to "make from herself a person." Within this female-centered focus, her themes were varied, and can best be understood as a series of related tensions, dichotomies, and ambivalences. (Yezierska had once complained, "My greatest tragedy in life is that I always see the two opposites at the same time." In retrospect, this ability to see two sides of an issue appears not as a tragedy but as the primary source of her writing's complexity and strength.) In much of Yezierska's fiction, there is the fierce drive to break away from the traditional Jewish family structure, a family that in many cases included a tyrannical father who expected his daughters to meekly sacrifice themselves for the economic good of others. But there is also guilt and a deep desire for familial, particularly paternal, approval. There is an attraction to Judaism's reverence for learning, its spiritualism, and its long history of faith and suffering, as well as a fascination with its romance, its status as a mystical link to the Old World. But there is also rage at the rigidity of Jewish tradition, where women were considered sinful by nature, inferior to men both spiritually and intellectually. There is the longing to be a financially independent single woman, free of a conventional husband's demands and control. But there is also desire for the pleasures of romance and marriage, for marriage's emotional and financial security. There is the delight and satisfaction in creative work, and there is the crushing necessity of earning money. There is the struggle with poverty, and there is a yearning for beauty in the midst of such deprivation. There is an intense attraction to the American marketplace, with its wealth of Americanizing commodities, and a revulsion for the marketplace's empty materialism. And in virtually every story and novel, there is the theme with which Yezierska is so often identified: the distance between the mythologized America, the "golden country" of legendary promise, and the often bitter reality of the immigrant experience—"America, as the oppressed of all lands have dreamed America to be, and America *as it is*."

Similarly, in many Yezierska stories, there is a strong Yiddish inflection, for the influence of Yiddish on her fiction contributed to more than her sentimental style. Capable of writing in grammatically correct, standard English, at many moments she employed awkward, Yiddish-influenced syntax, Yiddish phrases, and English translations of Yiddish expressions. She did so advisedly. By the time she was writing, the Yiddish language had attained respectability among Jewish intellectuals and artists; no longer considered a degraded tongue, it had become in many contexts the index of an authentic Jewish folk milieu. And while Yezierska's use of Yiddish did not result in the sort of poetic eloquence later achieved by Henry Roth's technique in *Call It Sleep,* her Yiddish inflection lends her prose the tone of a streetwise idiom. It is raw, vivid, and immediate, a style calculated, in Yezierska's words, to convey "the dirt and the blood of the poor." With *Arrogant Beggar,* we encounter far fewer Yiddishisms than in her earlier work. This serves to indicate the narrator's greater assimilation; unlike many protagonists in Yezierska's fiction, Adele Lindner has been born in America.

While it is important to register Yezierska's thematic and stylistic contributions to literature, such an academic account of her work risks overlooking her fiction's essential charm. Even those critical reviews that most reviled her work often admitted to a grudging admiration for the power of her prose. Indeed, the deep ambivalence of the critical reaction to *Arrogant Beggar* is striking; reviewers reacted negatively to the novel's subject matter and sentimental style, and yet were at a loss to account for their attraction to the text. The *New York Times* delivered a backhanded compliment, declaring, "It is a vividly told story, rushing pell mell from one episode to the next, seldom pausing for background, characterization, or detail of any sort beyond scattered essentials." Before haughtily denouncing Yezierska's lack of good taste, Marya Zaturenska at the *New York Herald Tribune* noted that she had "a fiery sincerity that is utterly moving," and declared, in a markedly mixed message, "In spite of its crudities, this is a strangely eloquent book." The reviewer for the *Saturday Review of Literature* began by relegating Yezierska to the ranks of the sentimentalists (noting that Yezierska was famous for speaking "the language of the emotions") and appeared to dismiss *Arrogant Beggar* according to the classic terms used against the sentimental: "The plot is trite, the characterization is thin, and the thought is an elaboration of the obvious"; "The faint pathos of a marionette show hovers about the volume." But the reviewer then admitted that the story was well told, even "exhilarating," with a "style [that] goes at lightning speed; the reader is whirled onward from sentence to sentence at a rate that for sheer thrill of movement hardly has its equal." In a statement that reads like a standard dismissal of female writers throughout history, the reviewer paid penance for this admission of pleasure by concluding, "She is not Shakespeare nor yet Cervantes, but she is pleasant to listen to, even when, as in the present volume, she has nothing particular to say."

If the critics were willing covertly to admit to the power of Yezierska's prose, they were not eager to recognize or endorse the radical critique that formed the basis of the novel's subject matter. It was not the first time she had addressed this sensitive issue. Throughout her work, Yezierska had assumed the perspective of the outsider to examine and critique America and American institutions. In several stories—"The Free Vacation House," "The Lord Giveth," "America and I," "My Own People," "How I Found America," "A Bed for the Night," *Salome of the Tenements*—she had decried the condescension of American philanthropies, charities, and settlement houses, their systematic humiliation of the charity recipient, their patronizing failure to understand the traditions of Jewish immigrants and the difficulties of survival in the ghetto. But although *Arrogant Beggar* is not Yezierska's first discussion of organized charity, it remains her most extensive and effective treatment of the subject, and the only text to address the institution of the charity-run boarding home.

At the time of *Arrogant Beggar*'s publication, the organized boarding home movement was an important influence on the urban landscape—as it had been since the late nineteenth century, when middle- and upper-class women first opened dozens of subsidized boarding houses for single working-class women. In contrast to the settlement houses which performed social work by serving as community centers, subsidized boarding homes were primarily dormitories; social work and education focussed on a target population rather than the community at large. And while only a small percentage of working women actually lived in such homes, the ideology behind the organized boarding home movement was a powerful determinant of how single working-class women were perceived by society. As the historian Joanne Meyerowitz has noted, the impetus behind the movement was intimately related to anxieties about the sexual vulnerability of young, unmarried working women. Arguing that these women were in need of protection from sexual assault and the conditions that might drive them to prostitution, the movement's founders rationalized the rigid system of rules and regulations enforced in most homes. By mobilizing a rhetoric that perpetuated an idealization of domesticity, the benefactors attempted to contain working women within the "safe" domestic sphere. In practice, this meant representing the boarding "home" as a haven from the evils of the street, portraying themselves as mother figures for the working "girls," and presenting marriage as the only feasible escape from the perils of economic survival.

But while the benefactors of the boarding homes explicitly depicted themselves as protectors of the working woman, another prevalent rhetoric of the era focused on a rather different matter: not society's threat to working women but the myriad threats posed by working women to society. This discourse took as its subject not a fear for working women's sexual vulnerability but an anxiety about working women's putatively opportunistic sexuality. Single working-class women, stereotyped as sexually available "gold diggers," might potentially tempt middle-class men to adultery, jeopardizing the sanctity of middle-class marriage. What is more, a working-class woman might succeed in marrying "up," catching a man of a higher class. Anxieties about class transgression by means of marriage were matched only by anxieties about class transgression through consumption: working-class women of the late nineteenth and early twentieth centuries were notorious for strategically manipulating commodities—chiefly clothing—to imitate the appearance of higher class women. For all of these reasons, single working-class women at large in the city seemed to threaten the system of class distinctions upon which many middle- and upperclass women depended for a sense of identity. In the face of such anxieties, the charity-run boarding home appeared an ideal space in which to attempt to contain and control working-class women. And rather than working to ameliorate the economic conditions that placed self-supporting women "at risk"—hazardous workplaces, low wages, irregular employment—the benefactors instead were often engaged in an effort to reconcile working-class women to working-class life. The power of Anzia Yezierska's *Arrogant Beggar* lies in its attention to such issues, its brilliant exposure of the class tensions inherent in this American charity tradition.

The first half of *Arrogant Beggar* follows the fortunes of the young narrator, Adele Lindner, as her early idealization of the Hellman Home for Working Girls turns into cynical disillusionment. Yezierska uses the first section of the novel to gradually reveal the negative features of boarding home life. In exposing the rigidity of the rules, the lack of privacy, the institutional ambiance, and the residents' lack of control over their food and surroundings, Yezierska articulates the criticisms typically made by actual boarding home residents. But these drawbacks, although annoying, are not what ultimately alienate Adele. Her disenchantment comes when she recognizes the stunning philosophy behind the philanthropy of the Home's benefactors. Adele's visit to the Hellman mansion serves as the first stage of this disenchantment. While Adele sees in Mrs. Hellman a friend and a mentor, Mrs. Hellman regards Adele as a mendicant who must be reminded of her place. Adele wishes to elevate herself materially and intellectually, but Mrs. Hellman is concerned only that Adele adjust herself to her low social position. Extolling the virtues of poverty, Mrs. Hellman argues that Adele must learn to love drudgery and toil and must humbly do her part to maintain the status quo, to preserve "the harmony and perfection of the whole universe." Finally, it is Mrs. Hellman's deliberate physical rejection of Adele, the act of wiping Adele's kiss off her cheek, that initiates Adele's painful realization of the power differential upon which charity is predicated, the underlying inequities of the class system. "Why should they have the glory of giving and we the shame of taking like beggars the bare necessities of life?"

The second stage of Adele's rude awakening comes as she is working as a serving maid at a luncheon for the benefactors of the Home. Eavesdropping on the conversation, she hears the wealthy women declare that "the besetting vices of the working class are discontent and love of pleasure," and that working women must "adjust" themselves to the conditions in which they find themselves, must narrowly circumscribe all ambition. The conversation reveals the benefactors' overriding fear that the class hierarchy will be destabilized, that the working women's "appetites" will be "roused" through their experiences at the Home and they will acquire "notions of superiority." Yezierska deftly counterposes the benefactors' deep anxieties about the dress and appearance of the working women with the benefactors' own excesses and vanity in dress and jewelry. The scene serves as the centerpiece of Yezierska's exposure of the charity givers' hypocrisy, their pleasure at being able to exercise power over the poor.

Adele's disillusionment is complete when she learns that Mrs. Hellman is exploiting her services; under the guise of helping Adele, Mrs. Hellman is in fact paying her at a lower rate than is standard. Adele's subsequent public denunciation of the Home targets the benefactors' condescension, the self-loathing that it creates in the charity recipient, and the way such charity enforces class distinctions rather than abolishing them. "Gratitude you want? For what? Because you forced me to become your flunkey—your servant? Because you crushed the courage out of me when I was out of a job? Forced me to give up my ambition to be a person and learn to be your waitress?"

The arrogance of Adele Lindner's attack on her benefactors— and Yezierska's arrogance in writing *Arrogant Beggar*—may well have puzzled many American readers. The novel's epigraph sets the stage for this arrogance. Emerson's statement goes beyond the simple observation that receiving largesse threatens the self-reliance of the recipient. Emerson argues that it is a human tendency to feel entitled to receive from society intellectual, psychological, and spiritual sustenance. But while Emerson's use of the pronoun "we" suggests that this sense of entitlement is universal, it is crucial to understand that Yezierska's concept of entitlement may well have been very different from accepted American precepts regarding charity. Indeed, it is arguable that Yezierska's notion of charity was largely conditioned by the norms of Jewish tradition in the shtetl where she was born and spent her childhood.

According to the anthropologists Mark Zborowski and Elizabeth Herzog, in the close-knit shtetls of Eastern Europe there was great emphasis on *tsdokeh,* a Hebrew word that can be translated as "social justice." The ideology behind *tsdokeh* dictated that beneficent giving not be regarded as charity but as simple fairness. *Tsdokeh* encompassed all forms of charitable giving (material gifts as well as good deeds), and was expected of each member of the community at all stages of life, according to his or her resources. The highest form of *tsdokeh* was that which was given with kindness. Although it was admittedly greater to give than to receive (those who gave gained prestige on earth and honor in heaven), the charity recipient was to be spared humiliation. Gifts would be called loans (although there was no expectation that they would be repaid), and secret gifts or gifts that were anonymous were considered the best kinds of charity, for the giver was kind enough not to advertise the giving. According to this tradition, those who were impoverished had the right to ask for assistance, and Jews who were wealthy were under obligation to help. While those who begged were referred to derisively as *shnorers* (beggars), such figures nonetheless had an established position in the shtetl community. Indeed, the charity givers were in a sense dependent upon the charity recipients; without the beggars, the givers would not gain heavenly favor for their beneficence. Beggars in the shtetl therefore often displayed aggression, arrogance, and a sense of entitlement. Yezierska's use of the phrase "arrogant beggar" thus has deep resonance with Old World tradition.

If the shtetl tradition of charity makes Yezierska's rage at the American charity tradition more comprehensible, it also makes the ethnic and religious status of the Home's benefactors an important issue. The names of several of the charity givers—Hellman, Stone, Gordon, Gessenheim—might indeed be Christian (as the reviewer for the *New York Herald Tribune* assumed when she wrote that Yezierska displayed an "amusing ignorance of gentile minds"). But it is more likely that these are intended to be German Jewish names. German Jews, having arrived in the United States a generation earlier than Russian Jews, were frequently regarded as largely assimilated to American life, less religious than Russian Jews, and more affluent. (Whereas German Jews were stereotyped as "uptown" Jews, Russian Jews were "downtown" Jews.) If indeed the benefactors are Jews, then according to Yezierska's terms they are not good Jews. Far from discreetly assisting the needy, the philanthropists conspicuously advertise their charity work in the newspaper; in every way, these assimilated German Jews disregard the *tsdokeh* of Russian Jewish tradition. *Arrogant Beggar* can thus be interpreted not simply as an attack on the American charity system but also as registering the irrelevance of shtetl tradition to the lives of assimilated Jews in America. In the shtetl, the *tsdokeh* conception of charity was crucial to the survival of the community, joining the individual to the larger Jewish group. But in the United

States, the cohesive, insular conditions of the shtetl did not exist, and such communitarian ideals appeared impractical.

While the first half of *Arrogant Beggar* demonstrates the shortcomings of American charity, the second half of the novel is an attempt to present alternative solutions to the problem of poverty. Yezierska proposes two different models of humanitarian assistance, both of which can be interpreted as efforts to reinsert the communitarian ideals of *tsdokeh* into urban life. The first model comes in the form of the philanthropy practiced by the old ghetto woman, Muhmenkeh. In contrast to the disciplinary, punitive "Big Sistering" of the socialites, who practice a patronage predicated on an unequal relationship between giver and receiver, Muhmenkeh models an egalitarian nurturance. She displays a willingness to accept gifts from the community as eagerly as she gives them; it is this bond of mutuality, of almost familial interdependence, that creates a "home feeling in the heart" for Adele. Indeed, Muhmenkeh serves as an idealized mother figure—the most idealized maternal presence in Yezierska's fiction—and is a character that signals a shift away from Yezierska's traditional focus on the tyrannical patriarch.

If Muhmenkeh presents one alternative to official charity, Adele herself presents another. After Muhmenkeh's death, Adele finds herself inspired by the old woman's spirit of generosity. She resolves to practice her own brand of humanitarian assistance to the ghetto community: she converts Muhmenkeh's basement apartment into a coffee house, serving the comforting foods of Jewish tradition, *mohn kuchen* and *gefülte fish*. The restaurant is an attempt to go beyond the contingencies of the capitalist marketplace, to insert communitarian ideals into American life. The success of the business is crucially dependent upon Adele's trust in the community, for customers pay at their own discretion, according to their ability. And, in accordance with the novel's epigraph, Adele's philanthropy accommodates not only physical needs but also intellectual, psychological, and spiritual hunger: her coffee house is a cultural center, complete with paintings on the walls, poetry recitals, and piano concerts. With the success of this alternative model of philanthropy, Adele avenges herself on her former benefactors. In succeeding, Adele has disregarded Mrs. Hellman's injunction that she stay in her place. And in a very real sense, she has fulfilled the benefactors' secret fear: her stay at the Home and her exposure to the bourgeois household through her position as a servant have taught her valuable lessons about commodities and the aesthetics of class.

Throughout much of her fiction, Yezierska had been fascinated by the commodity codes of class membership, the way a class affiliation is partially performed through "taste," a knowledge of distinctions between commodities. In the beginning of *Arrogant Beggar,* Adele longs for refinement through contact with material objects, and senses the cultural value of expensive commodities. "How much finer, more sensitive the Hellmans must be than plain people—they with so much beauty around them every day of their lives." Despite Adele's dislike of the domestic science course she took at the Home, the class ultimately—and ironically—helps her to master the bourgeois art of presentation. In endowing her basement café with a cultured, European ambiance, Adele has used the norms of taste and upper-class aesthetic distinctions for her own ends.

Yezierska's extended polemic on charity and class issues prompted one critic to accuse her novel of being nothing more than a "social survey document." Yet *Arrogant Beggar* is first and foremost a work of fiction. In choosing to frame her social critique according to the conventions of the sentimental romance, Yezierska was able to invest her text with emotional force. But her use of the romantic formula also led to a number of other consequences, particularly with respect to the novel's troubling stance on female identity and marriage. *Arrogant Beggar* at first appears to be a feminist revision of the "working-girl" romances that were published in story papers and dime novels in the late nineteenth and early twentieth centuries. According to the "working-girl" genre, the female protagonist was a friendless waif ultimately rescued from her poverty by a good-hearted upper-class man. In depicting Adele's early, tough-minded dismissal of romantic myths—"If you must have love and are poor—read about it in novels"—and in portraying Adele's rejection of Arthur Hellman's condescending offer of marriage, Yezierska appears to rewrite this formula. Nevertheless, the novel remains implicated in the conventions of romance. Adele's experiences throughout the novel are structured according to an equation whereby several suitors must be considered and rejected before true love is attained. Like the protagonists of *Bread Givers* and *Salome of the Tenements,* Adele forsakes her independence and marries by the conclusion of the novel. Moreover, Adele's relationship to Jean Rachmansky is highly traditional; her role consists in supporting and encouraging her husband's genius.

If *Arrogant Beggar* were to conclude on the day of Adele's marriage to Jean, the novel would indeed be locked into the romance script. The sentimental romantic form, which lent such rhetorical power to Yezierska's transgressive attack on the charity system, would seem to ultimately eclipse any political message, enforcing an obligatory depoliticizing, amnesia-inducing happy ending. But in fact the novel does not end there. Defying genre expectation in the last paragraphs, the text suddenly moves from the florid language of the newlyweds' passion to Adele's disquieting admission of anxiety. She has decided to repay Muhmenkeh, both literally and symbolically, by assisting Muhmenkeh's granddaughter to come to America. But in so doing, Adele has also crossed to the other side, become a benefactor, a Lady Bountiful. She can only watch and wait for young Shenah Gittel's inevitable ambivalence to this form of charity. The novel ends in a moment of suspended anticipation, as Jean and Adele stand on the gangplank, searching for Shenah. The young woman's face, appearing in the crowd, is in a sense the resurfacing of the social content of the novel, the return of what the novel's romantic formula appeared to repress with Adele and Jean's marriage.

We can read this moment as marking the site of Yezierska's struggle, as she fashions an imperfect reconciliation between the novel's radical content and its conservative form. In this moment's ambiguity, we see why the critics could not finally account for the novel's lingering effect, its strange eloquence. The novel's political content resonates precisely because it is presented in a form that ultimately eludes tidy categorization; it is neither a straightforward social tract nor a simple romance. We have in *Arrogant Beggar*'s unsettling conclusion striking evidence of the rich complexity that draws us, again and again, to the work of Anzia Yezierska.

Arrogant Beggar

To my friend Ruth Hester

"We do not quite forgive a giver.
The hand that feeds us is in some danger of being
bitten. We can receive anything from love, for that is a
way of receiving it from ourselves; but not from any one who
assumes to bestow. . . . We ask the whole. Nothing less will
content us. We arraign society, if it do not give us besides
earth, and fire, and water, opportunity, love,
reverence, and objects of veneration."

—Emerson

Chapter One

I was up before it was light. My hand felt under my pillow for the newspaper. It was a real story. Not just another one of my dreams. The first *real* way out of my black life.

I jumped into my shoes, started the coffee, reached for my comb—all in one breath. Gone the ache of a night on that ungodly bed. The sagging spring, the humpy, lumpy mattress. The smells from the fish store below no longer mattered.

Two swallows of coffee—and I was out, running down the street, clutching a roll in one hand, the magic newspaper in the other.

I couldn't stop my rush till I got on the steps of the house. I glanced at my wrist watch. Before seven. The street was still asleep. The late Sunday morning sleep. A whole hour yet before I dared ring the bell.

My reflection in the plate-glass door made me laugh in spite of all my excitement. My tam pulled over one ear, my thick red hair standing out on the other side like a wild Indian's. The bottom of my coat uneven, my collar awry because I had skipped the first buttonhole.

"Adele Lindner!" I laughed aloud, "what a funny little object you are!"

I set my hat in place, rebuttoned my coat, walking up and

down before the silent house. Again I turned to the article in the Sunday paper.

Mrs. Hellman, the banker's wife, had just given a hundred thousand dollars to endow the Home for Working Girls. . . . I looked at the pictures. Mrs. Hellman. What a face! The sunshine and goodness of the other world smiled at me. . . . Dining room—Gymnasium—Laundry. Even a reception hall where girls could invite men.

Imagine me inviting a man at Mrs. Greenberg's! Where? In her shut-up parlour? Her kitchen, where she watched every step made on her precious new oilcloth? Or in that hole in the wall—my bedroom?

If I wanted any of the men that wanted me—what would I do? They'd have to meet me in the street.

Here was *real home*. A place where a girl had a right to breathe and move around like a free human being. Everything I longed for and dreamed of at Mrs. Greenberg's was here. Light, air, space, enough room to hang up my clothes. Even a bureau with a mirror to see myself as I dressed. But more than the mirror, the space to move around. More than the light, the air. I wanted to meet that warm-hearted spirit of love who had thought it all out: Mrs. Hellman, the Friend of the Working Girl.

Spreading the newspaper on the cold stone steps, I sat down to wait. I leaned my head against the door, envious of the lucky girls safe inside.

Free! Free at last from the Mrs. Greenbergs, with the lodgings they kept, and the life they led me.

How she had nagged that time I had spattered a little water on the floor! Everything I had done that day got on Mrs. Greenberg's nerves. My milk had boiled over on *her* newly polished stove. I had left the gas burning in my room when I went down to the store. I had hung up the dishpan on the wrong hook. She found a scorched spot on the ironing board and blamed me for it.

I fled from her kitchen, not caring where I was going. In the dark hall I stumbled over a pail of suds with which Mrs. Hershbein, the janitress, was mopping the floor.

"Oi-i weh-h! Did you hurt yourself?" she cried, helping me up.

"Hell itself can't hurt me, since I live with Mrs. Greenberg," I laughed bitterly. "Eight dollars a month rent I pay her—and she makes me feel like a thief when I have to step into her kitchen."

"For your good money, why don't you look yourself around for another place?"

"What's another place? Last time I had a kind landlady. So the house was dirty, and now my landlady is so clean she stands at the kitchen door with a rag in her hand, waiting for me to wipe my shoes before I step on her new oilcloth."

"*Nu—nu,* Adele!" soothed Mrs. Hershbein. "Better come and give only a step up by me. A taste from my *gefülte* fish will make you forget your troubles."

Upstairs, in the corner of the kitchen, books all around him, was her son Shlomoh. His shabby pushcart clothes faded as his face lighted with intelligence. He stood up awkwardly, fidgeting with his necktie. "You!" he gulped. "I wanted to stop you—many times. I—you never noticed me. I saw you every day—" His voice came to a sudden halt. It made me nervous, the way he kept his eyes on me.

"In Columbia College he studies—my son," his mother pointed to him triumphantly. "Think only! In another year, he finishes himself—Doctor of Philosophy."

From the stove came the smell of *gefülte* fish and fried potato *lotkes*. Shlomoh joined his mother in insisting that I stay with them for dinner.

There, while drinking tea, after dinner, Shlomoh jestingly showed me the article in the Sunday paper about Mrs. Hellman. And here I was—on the doorsteps of the Hellman Home at last!

Eight o'clock pealed from the Metropolitan tower. My heart thumped in my ears as I pressed the bell.

A girl like myself opened the door. I caught a glimpse of the dining room. Long white tables, crowded with more girls like myself. Girls of my own kind, lively as at a party.

The office to which I was shown was as perfect as the picture in the paper. White Swiss curtains. Plain brown rug on the hardwood floor. The couch with cushions to match. My! What a difference from Mrs. Greenberg's parlour! Her lace curtains! The clutter of ornaments on the mantelpiece! The pink paper flowers in their five-and-ten-cent crystal vases! After that ugliness, what a relief it was just to breathe the quiet air of this uncrowded room!

Prominently on the wall was the portrait of a lady, Mrs. Hellman, the founder of the Home. Quietly I stood, raised my eyes to the beaming, gracious face. "Bless you—bless you"—the words said themselves like a prayer.

An important-looking woman came in. Her clothes were so neat, so smoothly pressed out on her figure. Like a model in our show window.

"Good-morning. What can I do for you, my dear?"

She walked over to a desk marked "Miss Simons" and pointed to a chair beside it.

"You'd like to live here?"

As her quick eye went over me, I felt so self-conscious—my hands gripped the chair to stop blushing. All the things I had prepared to say to her fled under my feet. How could I put into words what the beauty, the quiet of this place meant to me?

She picked up from her desk a printed slip, dipped her pen in the ink. "I'll take your name and address. . . . You live with your parents?"

"I have nobody. My father died when I was ten and my mother when I was fourteen. Ever since I've knocked about among strangers."

"What was your father's nationality?"

"Polish. But I'm an American. Born in New York."

"What was your father's occupation?"

"He was a tailor. Oh, but not just a plain tailor. He wanted to be a singer. That's why he came to America. He thought here everybody could learn what they wanted. He got stung, though. Had to keep right on with his tailoring. So crazy he was for music that—"

"Yes. Yes." Miss Simons interrupted. "How old are you?"

"I'm eighteen. But first I must tell you the way my father had to go to the opera every Saturday night, even when he robbed himself of his lunch money a whole week for it. Such a voice he had! I still remember, way inside of me, the way he sang *Pagliacci*—"

"What work do you do? How much do you earn?"

"I'm a saleslady in Bloomberg's Bargain Store. I get nine dollars a week. From eight in the morning till nine at night."

"My dear! What long hours!" She looked at me again. "One would never believe it. We'll have to get you a better job so you can keep your freshness."

This home. A better job. This woman for my friend! Through her—Mrs. Hellman!

"Oh, could I move in right away?"

"We'll have to investigate your references. It will require at least a month."

"A month? A whole month? How could I wait that long?"

"Child! Do be a little calmer. You'll wear yourself out if you go on that way."

"I can't be calm if I have to go back to Essex Street."

"Patience! A little patience!"

"Oh, if you knew what finding a person like you means to me! I've been so lonely—a lost animal—not a human being. . . . If I could only tell you how I always dreamed of home—white curtains, red and green geraniums, just like this. And the heart of it— a friend like you!"

"Well, Miss Lindner, you certainly have a way with you." She smiled. "But, after all, it's for girls like you that Mrs. Hellman endowed this institution."

She rose and patted my hand encouragingly. "I can assure you I'll do my best to hasten the investigation. You'll hear from me as soon as possible."

"I'm afraid to go away." I clung to her hand. "Suppose your letter should get lost? Are you sure you won't forget about me, with all your great work?"

"Oh, no, my child! I make it a point never to neglect the *individual*." She withdrew her hand, pulled out a drawer of cards. "You see? We are very systematic here. All our cases are filed, numbered, and card-catalogued. We keep a record of all our applications. This red clip over your card means special attention."

All the way back, it was as though the sun were shining in my eyes. But, nearing Essex Street, I saw again the houses huddled together in neglect, like a poor, over-crowded family. On either side of the stoop, rubbish, bags bursting and overflowing, two alley cats pulling the dirt out on the sidewalk.

The cracked doors on broken hinges. The cellar windows stuffed with rags. Over this ugliness, my new life beckoned. Oh, those shining knobs on the doors! Those sparkling windows. The very sidewalks scrubbed like marble floors.

"Well, Adele! How was the place?" Shlomoh ran toward me. Then stood gulping in confusion.

His mother waved at me from the stoop. "You look as if you won a fortune on the lottery."

"I have. That Hellman Home. The kindest woman on earth is in charge of it. Promised me better work. Already interested in me. Already my friend. *Think of it!*"

Shlomoh tried to smile. "You deserve to have it better. You belong in the sunshine, but we'll be so lonesome."

He reached for my hand.

I couldn't answer him. I turned to his mother, tucked my arm through hers as we picked our way up the dark stairs. "How I hate to think of leaving you here."

"*Nu, nu.* Each one finds his happiness in his own way. You're young yet. You need things. You're glad with your new home. I'm glad when I drink in pleasure from my Shlomoh. Soon he'll finish Doctor of Philosophy. What greater honor can I have in this world than to have a son, a learned man, a Doctor of Philosophy?"

"*Shah mammeniu!*" Shlomoh gave his mother a little teasing shove. "Once you said that Father was the greatest man that had ever been. Now it's your son. Little, vain *mammeniu!* The joke on you is that, if Father was great, it was because you carried him on your back, as you carry me."

Mrs. Hershbein did not attempt to answer such talk.

13

"*Nu!* Come in, only, children. The dinner is in a minute almost ready," she said, shooing us in before her.

How poor it all was. I never realized before how the rungs of the chairs were tied with ropes, the clutter of things on the bureau, the torn market bag with the spilling potatoes, bread and herring thrown on the bed. Everything so smelly, so dingy, and they unaware of it all.

Mrs. Hershbein fried a few pieces of fat with onions to put a meat taste into the barley soup, while I began to set the table. The old red tablecloth, limp, from many washings, felt thin and worn in my hands. The fringes barely clinging in spots like the last wisps of hair on a bald head.

I glanced at Shlomoh's pile of papers on the table. "What's all this writing about?"

"My column for the *New Light*. I've got to get it out tonight to have it in time for publication."

"And think only," broke in the mother proudly, "the way he works and works, and he don't want no pay."

"It's an educational magazine," he explained. "They don't pay any of their contributors."

I looked at his stooped shoulders, the baggy, shapeless clothes. Not caring how he looked—what he wore! If his mother forgot to feed him, he'd forget to eat. If she didn't put the shoes on his feet, he'd go barefoot and never know it. Even when he is a Doctor of Philosophy, he'll never be anything but a *Melamid* like his father, who spent his days poring over old, musty books, learning and learning—for the next world.

"The grass will grow on you if you don't look out for yourself," I scolded.

He looked up and laughed. "Well, Adele, if it does, I'll never be able to sell it for hay. A business man I'll never be. Money I'll never make. Something in me is just as it was with my father."

"But look where he left you. Do you want to remain always in a back-alley janitor's flat?"

"If I had to earn the rent for better rooms, buy myself a new suit every year, it would take me away from all my work."

"Where will your work get you? Have you no ambition?"

"Ambition? Don't you see how I'm just eating myself up only to learn?"

For a moment, I was awed by the spirit in him. His shabby clothes didn't matter. There was a look in his face that made me ashamed of wanting the comforts of the Hellman Home.

"You think my father had no ambition? Tearing himself out of his sleep in the chill of the early morning, hurrying to the synagogue. If you could have seen his eyes as he rocked back and forth over the Talmud, hours upon hours, days upon days, years upon years. My father and a whole lot of other men like my father. My race—yours, too—crazy to learn, to learn, to know."

"And when you know everything you want to know, what then?"

"I'll work to make things better."

I smiled as I saw Shlomoh again as he was. A round-shouldered *Melamid* with torn shoes, patched elbows, dreaming he could "make things better."

"His father, may he rest in peace, was just the same." Mrs. Hershbein beamed with pride in her men. "To work for himself, to make for himself an easier life, never came into his head. His life, his pleasure, his everything was to sit down with his books and learn. Wait, only, till he finishes Doctor of Philosophy. Then he'll settle himself and get married."

15

"A Doctor of Philosophy is wonderful. But how can he ever get married when he don't think of making a living?"

"God sends always to the spinner his flax, to the drinker his wine, and to the man that is a learner, the wife that will help him go on with his learning. Though I came from a rich father's house, I cooked and washed, tended a little grocery store, and even had time enough to bring my husband his dinner in the synagogue."

I loved her because she gave up so much of herself. But I knew I could never, never be like that.

But Mrs. Hershbein and Shlomoh were forgotten as I hurried back to my room. Out came my things from the boxes under the bed. I stayed up until I heard the next-door roomer stumble in from his night work at the shop. Darning stockings, ironing collars, patching the sleeves of my one serge dress, ready to move.

Too excited to sleep, I crawled out on the fire escape, drawn to the little patch of gray which was all the sky I ever saw between the black hulks of the tenements. The gray began to glow. Morning was breaking.

A moment of silence with nothing to mar the beauty. Then a cloud of black soot from a factory chimney darkened the glow of morning. The crash of the elevated trains, factory whistles, rumbling trucks, and the thousand and one noises that begin the day swept away my thoughts.

How could the soul keep alive here—where every breath of beauty was blotted out with soot, drowned in noise—where even the sky was a prisoner and the stars choked?

Chapter Two

The last day at Mrs. Greenberg's! So frantic I was to get away from the old place. And yet—I paused in the packing. My eyes filled with the dishevelled room. I have lived here. . . . This splintered floor, these mouldy pieces of ceiling were invisible eyes, watching day and night everything going on in me. They knew the inmost silences beneath my thoughts.

My hand caressed the torn wall, as if it were a living part of me. I felt I was leaving something of myself behind.

Poor, stingy Mrs. Greenberg! The last moment, I felt so sorry for her, I gave her all the things I couldn't use any more. My broken cup, my old hat, and best of all, my green, faded, ten-cent-a-yard curtains.

Gee! It felt great to be a benefactor! How I'd love to give if I had things.

"Why have the poor such generous hearts?" I asked Shlomoh, as he helped me fasten the straps of my satchel. "Even you should have a souvenir. I'll let you carry my bundles for me as a parting gift."

Shlomoh looked at me and smiled. He was in one of his silent moods. Not a word till we got to the door of the Home.

"May you only live here in good luck," he said solemnly. His

eyes searched the building from side to side, from roof to basement. "Ramparts of philanthropy! Even the walls look down at
you."

"Don't you like it, Shlomoh?"

"It's a grand place, Adele. But the solid righteousness of its
stone front—" he broke off, and added gently: "God forbid I
should spoil your happiness. I was only thinking how lonesome I'll
be without you."

"Lonesome? With your books, your *New Light,* and all the
people of the earth to educate and make better?"

A little wry smile came over his face. He held out his hand.
"Don't forget what I told you. When you're tired of chicken and
ice cream, you're welcome to come back and have *gefülte* fish with
Mother and me."

I saw him turn, look back twice over his shoulder. His eyes still
followed me as I walked slowly up the steps.

The next moment Shlomoh was forgotten. Every bit of me
was feeling forward. I drew myself up with all the life that was in
me, breathed in the new air, and rang the bell.

I felt the sun must stand still in high heaven. The whole world
must stop—to see the triumphant entrance of Adele Lindner into
the Hellman Home.

I showed my card of admission to the girl in the office. "Please
tell Miss Simons—I've come—to live here."

"She's at a committee meetin'. Wait in there," came from the
girl indifferently. "I'll find out where to put you."

Where to put me? Suppose there was no place for me, after all!
I clutched my bundles, looking about with frightened eyes for
someone to appeal to. There—on the wall—Mrs. Hellman's portrait smiled down at me. Thank God! I sank into a chair. The

dread and the worry dropped with the bundles to the floor. They wouldn't put me out with *her* here.

Through the open door, I saw girls coming in from work. Some slumped, tired, pale. Others bright and eager for the evening ahead. What lively times I would soon be having! I longed to run over to them, catch them by the hands.

A firm, quick step came from the hall. "Are you the new girl? I'm the matron. Come. I'll show you to your room."

She pushed a key into the lock, threw open a door. "Here we are! This will be your bed," she said, patting away a tiny wrinkle in the very smooth bedspread. And she was gone.

There were three chairs in the room. I had to try each one of them in turn. I was just getting up from the last chair when the door opened. A girl with tired eyes dropped heavily on the bed.

"God Almighty!" she burst out. "How I hate Christmas! Only a chance to work us to death for nothing!" She flopped back on the bed like a dead lump.

I was still gasping at the strangeness of this girl when in came my other roommate. "Hello! I was just beginning to enjoy it two in a room, but it was too good to last. Trala-la-la . . ."

"My! With all those windows full of air—and three separate beds! Why, a dozen girls could live in comfort here."

"You're good, kid," she laughed. "I'm glad you're not a gloomy Gus like that nut over there."

We were friends at once.

"How long are you gonna stay? I've been here already a year and a half. But soon there'll be someone else in my place, you bet. See? That's my engagement ring. Say, Sadie Silverstein—you lazy lummox," she scolded the heap on the bed. "Can't you do nothing but lie there? Look! There's somebody new in the room."

Not receiving any answer, she turned to me again. "What's your name?"

"Adele Lindner."

"And mine is Minnie Rosen—only for a little while yet, soon it'll be Mrs. Sam Sopkin." She flashed her ring again.

"Say! You got a beau?" she giggled.

"Dozens," I flung back. "Why? You want a change?"

"Go on! Quit your kiddin'! Is he pash'?"

I looked at her without speaking.

"Does he jingle the pockets? Shove you the gold?"

"He gave me these books." I began to take them out. She read the titles, *Crime and Punishment, Resurrection, Poor People.*

"What dumb stuff!"

The girl on the bed began to stir. One leg moved, than an arm. Then Sadie Silverstein dragged the rest of herself up, leaning on her elbow. "Awh-h-h! What a fuss they make buying and buying presents! Whoever bought me yet a present with all the Christmas crushes I saw through."

"Stop letting out your blues on us," came from Minnie impatiently. She pulled me over to the closet. "Say, kid! You can use those hangers. It's gonna be crowded as hell with three in here. Hope you haven't much stuff. I don't wanna get my new dress all wrinkled."

I took off my hat, hung up my things in the closet. Minnie stared at me in a friendly way. "Gee! I wish I had your hair. Such bunches of it. You can keep your freckles, though. And I don't care about being so skinny. But honest to God! When you take off that black hat—oh, boy!" And Minnie raised her brows and rolled her eyes.

Miss Simons came in just as I shoved my bag under the bed.

"So here you are, my dear. We are glad to welcome you a member of our Home. Have you met your roommates—Sadie Silverstein, Minnie Rosen—Tired again, Sadie? Another hard day?" Then, her eye falling on Sadie's dirty shoes, she added quietly: "Wouldn't you be more comfortable if you took your shoes off before you lay down on the white bedspread?" In the same controlled voice, she turned to me: "My dear, didn't I notice that you shoved your things under the bed? We don't permit bags or trunks in the room. There's a nice place in the basement for them. . . . Oh, yes—and about the rules—see, they're tacked there on the door. Be sure to read them carefully."

As Miss Simons disappeared, I cried out: "How can I get on without my bag?"

A twinkle came into Sadie Silverstein's lifeless eyes. "Cheer up! Worse things are yet to come."

"I guess you're yet a little green to these here 'Homes,' " added Minnie.

With puzzled look I turned to the card on the door:

Rules of the Home

I read and read. "Goodness! Why do they need so many rules?"

"You'll soon find out. Then you'll know why I'm so crazy to get married," said Minnie.

The dinner bell.

Like hundreds of chattering sparrows, the girls crowded into the dining room. The smell of steaming potatoes and fried liver! Waitresses in white aprons to serve the girls as though they were ladies in a hotel. How exciting that first meal was!

Someone was saying, "Pleased to meet you." I must have been

introduced to that dark girl, blinking at me through thick glasses. "That's Angela Patruno. Works in a pants factory. Ain't she a cute little wop?"

My roommate pointed out a pale-faced blonde with red-lidded eyes. "She's a sample-maker in an embroidery shop. Her name's Maria Rezienska—a Pollack just outa Ellis Island."

A fat girl with a bright blue beaded waist and a string of pink pearls talked all the time. "Oh, mamma! What swell gowns in that new Norma Talmadge picture!" What furs! What hats! She sure has some style. . . ."

The waitress put a plate down before me. Liver, fried onions, and mashed potatoes in neat little piles. Like a regular plate dinner in a restaurant.

But Minnie Rosen turned up her nose. "Liver again! And tough as leather!"

"Thank the Lord, it's liver. They only give us that once a week. It's that eternal hash and hamburger that gets me. God knows what they put into it."

An Irish girl with blue eyes and black hair roared with laughter. "Faith, you kids! It's at the Waldorf you think you are. When I was with them Sisters, no feller could cross the door-step. No fellers, no pettin'—gawd! That's worse 'n bad eats."

"Not for mine," grumbled Minnie Rosen. "I can't live on lovin'."

"You kikes are always kicking."

"And you wops—macaroni suckers."

"Dry up! Hollering and fighting like a League of Nations. Kikes, Wops, Micks, and Polacks. Only thing missing's a Chink to make it perfect."

Their complaints dwindled into a faint discontented murmur as Miss Simons passed on her way to her own table.

"There goes our deficit," someone buzzed behind her hand.

"You see old Simons, there?" Sadie added, under her breath. "We call her our 'deficit.' That means we're on charity. Because you think Simons eats what we eat? No. Chops and beefsteak for her. Spring lamb and gracious knows what."

I swallowed everything on my plate. The liver tasted better than anything I could cook for myself on Mrs. Greenberg's stove. I wondered from what rich homes they came if they could pretend to complain of such good eating. As for Miss Simons, why shouldn't she have the best? She was so kind, so good. How could anyone help wanting her to have anything but the best?

"Say, kids! Here's a joke on old Simons!" Minnie giggled. "The old girl sent a letter to my boss to find out how much I earn. But you think he told her the truth? You bet your life he didn't. I told him to say just half what I really earn. Whatever we pay here is too much. It's charity, anyhow."

The girls broke into little screams of laughter. "Better keep your money for your hope chest."

"I'd get married to-night if Sam didn't have to wait for his raise. The idea of having to report to that old maid every time my own fellah wants me out a little later at a dance."

"She's only jealous because the men give her the go-by."

"Nobody is holding us here by force," I had to speak up. "Tell me a boarding house where we could get such food, such clean, airy rooms for the money we pay?"

"Look at the new girl!"

"What's the big idea! How did you get that way?"

23

"Sure, she's right. The ladies of the board won't shed any tears if any of us leave."

"I'm not kicking at the grub—though old Simons ought to be made to eat the stuff she thinks good enough for us. But it's the high-hat stuff that gets my goat. It's the fat mammas giving the glad hand to poor little sister."

"And their pat-me-on-the-back leaves me cold—knocks me dead."

What a thankless lot these girls were! Instead of being warmed by the beauty of this place, they sit back with the coldness of superior ladies, looking for black spots on the sun. God! Wasn't it ever possible to satisfy poor people? What more do they want?

Were they showing off before me? Dissatisfied? Such a grand place! Such a good meal! Imagine being so happy that you could play at being ill-treated.

After dinner, the girls drifted into the Social Hall. Minnie dashed over to the piano and began pounding out *Dearie, My Dearie*. Some stood around the piano, their arms about each other, singing shrilly. Others broke into couples. The room swayed with the whirling colours of the dancing girls.

Minnie, with her flame-coloured blouse, her diamond ring, her stylishly curled hair, bounced and jerked to the jazz she hammered out on the piano.

Goldie glided around as in a dream. Silent, cheek to cheek, with a far-off look in her eyes. In perfect step with her partner. Anyone could see she was thinking of her man as she danced.

Two girls tried out a new tango with shrieks of laughter.

"Hey, there! How about looking where you're going? That's the second hunk you've taken out of my patent leathers."

"Say, popper! Look at Yetta shake the wicked hip!"

"Gimme the next one, Yetta!"

"Oh, hot lips!"

"Come to me, kid! Nothing makes me sick!"

How wonderful it all was. The pounding jazz. The shuffling feet. The joy flowing through their swaying bodies.

Sadie Silverstein, the only girl who didn't join in the fun. She sat back against the wall with a face like a funeral. Suddenly I grabbed hold of her, leaped into a Hester Street jig.

In a minute they were all around us, clapping and stamping!

"Say! Look at the Red-Head!"

"Baby! What eyes! See the spark fly!"

"Oh, boy! Watch her kick the pebbles!"

"Even Sadie Gloom twinkles in her light!"

We gave it to them livelier and livelier. We were little rough-necks of the tenements, dancing free and wild in front of the street organ.

Chapter Three

How I loved those first days at the Home! The exciting experience of lying down on a smooth mattress between two fresh, clean sheets. For the first time free from the stuffy old featherbeds, dank with the smell of dead generations.

Long after Minnie and Sadie were asleep, I was still wide awake, luxuriating in that bed. My body opened a million mouths of famine, sucking in thirstily the softness of wool blankets, the freshness of it all. . . . Heaven must be a white place like a clean white sheet. . . .

The waking gong at six in the morning rang and rang till the sleepiest girl jumped up and began rushing. Bathing. Dressing. Making the beds. Tidying the room. The strict shutting of the dining-room door at the second of seven-thirty.

At night, the bell to get back to your room. Perfect quiet. Lights out. Each and all part of that soldier's routine.

But what slips I made before I learned to keep step!

One day, after work, I had to buy some stockings. I walked into store after store. "You have black stockings for twenty-nine cents?"

"Forty-nine cents is the cheapest," everyone said.

It took me nearly an hour to go all the way back to Essex Street. But there I got my twenty-nine-cent stockings at the first pushcart.

Hurrying along, I caught a dozen familiar smells. Herring, onions, pickled tomatoes standing in a row of wooden tubs. The stuffy streets without enough air to go around for all those crowds of people. Suddenly, as I stood wedged in between pushcarts, bargaining with the man to let me have a spool of cotton a penny cheaper, I was seized with the fear that all this clutter was still part of me. Perhaps I had never really been away from it all. Perhaps I had only dreamed that I was now living at the Home.

Quickly I paid the man the four cents. I was so scared I'd be sucked in this terrible dirt again, I ran.

Someone shook a dusty featherbed out of the window.

Something blew into my eye, nearly blinding me. Before I could find the nearest drug store, that speck of dust got so deep in my lid, the man had to spend a long time getting it out.

How glad I was to make my escape from those horrible streets!

I ran to make sure the clean feel of my new life was real. . . .

"It's real enough," I laughed to myself when I reached the Home and found the door locked. The house in darkness. Down on Essex Street the houses were always open.

With a keen sense of pleasure, I gave the bell a long, hard pull. I was tasting another flavour of respectability.

The matron, solid and stiff in her white starched uniform, opened the door. "Why are you ringing that way?" she frowned. "Here, put your name down in the late book."

"I got back as quick as I could. Why do they need late books?"

"The idea of questioning the rules of the house! I have a good mind to report you to Miss Simons." And turning to answer the doorbell, she admitted Miss Simons herself.

"Why, Adele! You? An hour late? I certainly never thought you'd be one of the girls to break the rules."

27

"What's the sense of having such a rule?"

"What a silly question! How can one run an institution without rules? Suppose the girls were allowed to come in at all hours of the night—what then?"

I told her of my accident and that I might not have been able to go to work the next day if I had not attended to my eye immediately.

"But you had no business to be out shopping so near the closing hour. You should have bought your things during your lunch time, as the other girls do. Rules are rules. Bear in mind, my dear, that you're not the only girl in this Home."

I wanted to answer, but the words stuck inside. I gripped the pen with tight fingers, scrawled my name.

Half the night I kept thinking, my name on record as a rule-breaker.

Never in my life had I known what it was to live by rules. I began to look back and wonder, wasn't I perhaps a little freer when I lived alone?

Freer? But then I thought of next Sunday. Miss Simons had announced we must prepare something extra fine for our next social. Those who had boy friends could invite them. And think of it! Mrs. Hellman herself was coming. At last I was to meet her—talk to her—my friend of friends!

"I'll bet she brings along her darling son, Arthur Hellman," whispered Minnie. "She never misses a chance to show him off."

"Mrs. Hellman has a son? How old is he? What does he look like?" I spilled out my eagerness.

"Don't you worry. She don't let none of us get near him. All we get is a look. A regular sheik. You'll faint away when you see him."

I drew in my breath. The coming social! Mrs. Hellman's son. The other world.

Life burst open a million doors and windows. Front rows in the theatre. Boxes in the opera. Dining in those elegant places with softened lights where music plays.

I invited Shlomoh Hershbein. But I kept thinking and dreaming how it would feel if I could have invited a man like Arthur Hellman. He was so clear before my eyes. Tall. Dark. Aristocratic.

If I could only make myself look a little better when I met him. I tried my hair a dozen different ways. I fussed with the few clothes I had, wondering which was most suitable. I tried on the tan blouse, then my blue. When I saw the cheap fancy styles of the girls, I decided on my plain black dress. The Hellmans must see at first sight that I was different from all the others.

A racket of voices sounded through the halls, laughing and shouting. The girls kept coming in and out, trying on one another's clothes, elbowing each other before the mirror.

"Say, Yetta! How does this look on me?"

"Gonna wear your lace collar? Will you leave me wear it for to-night?"

"Does this lipstick show too red?"

"Ain't you the little vamp!"

"Give only a look! How these beads shine up my neck!"

How excited they got dolling themselves up!

There was an edge to the fun that was not there when they were only girls. Underneath their chumminess, each girl hoped that the other would not look quite her best.

"Adele! Adele!" Someone called. "Your beau is waiting. You better hustle and come down, or they'll kidnap him on you!"

29

Poor Shlomoh! What a face! Lost in a wilderness of girls.

I introduced him to Minnie Rosen who sized him up in one glance.

"I'll bet you love dancing—*nit*."

Shlomoh stared at his tight new shoes. "I didn't know it was going to be a dance," he gulped nervously, swaying on his heels to rest his toes. "I only wanted to sit and talk with you."

"They're starting. We'll have time to talk later on."

We walked into the glittering dance hall. Young men with their girls paraded, looking each other over. The room was alive with a high-strung gaiety of girls in their holiday best. Their faces, their eyes, their laughter quickened by the stimulating sight of men.

But all these men were like the men I saw every day in the store, in the cars, going from work, coming from work. I wanted something different from my working world. My eyes searched every corner of the place for Arthur Hellman. The thrill of the evening hadn't begun because he was nowhere in sight.

A violin solo was followed by a song. After that Minnie played *Dearie, My Dearie.* Then the chairman explained that, because of illness, Yetta Blum would not recite. "Will someone volunteer in Yetta's place?"

The girls looked at one another, giggling nervously: "Go on, kid! Give them *You Made Me Love You.*"

An urge to stand upon the stage seized me. How I'd love to fire the crowd with my voice as Minnie did with her jazz!

"Are there any volunteers?" the chairman repeated.

"Me!" But as soon as I jumped up, I felt scared to death. I wished I were back at Mrs. Greenberg's. Too late.

"Step forward, please." The voice of the chairman felt like handcuffs on my wrists.

I felt myself moving without legs toward the platform. Upon the stage there was another black moment of terror. A blur of faces. My throat was dry. My tongue stuck in my mouth.

Without my will a poem I had long loved rang out:

> "Lord of my heart's elation,
>> Spirit of things unseen,
> Be Thou my aspiration,
>> Consuming and serene."

As I heard my voice fall upon the room, row after row of faces cleared. Clearer than all the others, I saw a man in the last row. He looked up at me with such friendly interest, almost as if he had reached out his hand to me. I knew it was Arthur Hellman. I grew surer and surer of myself. My voice rang out more and more triumphantly.

I saw the man turn to the lady beside him. They both looked at me with such pleasure that my heart swelled with happiness and power. I climbed to the top of my poem. Even I felt the thrill in my voice:

> "Bear up, bear out, bear onward,
>> This mortal soul alone,
> To selfhood or oblivion
>> Incredibly Thine own."

Stillness, then clapping.

Minnie Rosen rushed over, a crowd of girls after her.

"You're some speecher, kid! I got to hand it to you."

"Honest to God! You could melt away a heart of stone."

"The way you pushed out your eyes! You was like a close-up of Mary Pickford."

Through this loud, laughing nonsense, a gentle voice broke. "I'm Mrs. Hellman. It was a real pleasure to hear you, my dear." And while her hand still held mine, she added: "This is my son."

Mrs. Hellman herself introducing her son to me! In this triumphant moment I forgot her—looking at him.

He was not dark. His hair was smooth and brown. But he was tall and slender and breathed the other world.

He shook hands, too. And I was no more on earth.

"Good for you. I enjoyed it immensely."

The way he looked at me, I felt as if that far-off world of his held out its arms. Everything in me rushed out in response to that friendly smile. Then he and his mother moved on.

"You were glorious," Shlomoh whispered. "A man would give you dove's milk to drink if he'd only see the shine in your eyes."

The girls, hot and excited, still crowded around me. But I didn't know what it was all about. Everything in me went cold. What was the use of their telling me how wonderful I was if I couldn't make *him* stay any longer than that?

"Let's go for a walk," I said to Shlomoh. "I'm choking for air."

Out on the steps. Suddenly, I was all fire and excitement again. Below us at the curb was Arthur Hellman. He helped his mother into the car. He followed and shut the door.

I was staring so hard, I stumbled on the step and had to grab at Shlomoh's arm to steady myself.

He pulled me closer to him, his eyes shining. It got on my nerves. What business was it of his to be glad about me!

32

"It's a wonderful night," Shlomoh breathed, his hand stealing around my waist.

"Don't touch me!" I drew back stiff as wood.

"Adele!—I—I—thought—" He stopped suddenly. And we walked around the block in dumb, heavy silence.

There was a hurt reserve in his good-bye. And hurt was in his awkward slouch as he slipped away.

I was glad Minnie and Sadie were asleep when I got to my room.

I lay in bed wide awake. Shlomoh was a clumsy _yok_, Arthur Hellman the most thrilling man on earth. I was all wings and air, fire and longing, trying to hold that polite, distant, friendly smile of his.

Unapproachable. A god, standing in a museum, with the sign, "Don't Touch." Looking out with his cool gaze at the crowd around him.

"Sea-gray eyes," I whispered to myself, under the covers. "Not dark, but those queer, gray-green glints of colour, more distinguished than dark. Eyes shading in with the smooth, mouse-brown hair."

The first man of the other world. The first man I must know. But how can I open that shut door? How make him see me the next time we meet?

new world
Arthur Hellman
unattainable

old world
Shlomoh
decent man

33

Chapter Four

And then—the bottom dropped out from under my feet. I lost my job. After the holiday rush business went dead in the store.

I stood at my counter all day like a policeman alone on his beat. No one came near me. No one wanted gloves or neckwear now that all the Christmas presents had been given.

First one girl was laid off. Then another.

Then the boss came over with the bad news. "A live wire like you," he finished, "with your smart head—you can get another job in no time."

I started looking for work in other stores. Even in the shops and factories, it was the slack season.

Day after day, I got up in the early hours of the morning, and searched through the ads. It was Friday of the third week, and no job.

I watched the few dollars I had melt away in my hands, for carfares, newspapers, and stamps. But, even in my panic, there was thankfulness that I was no longer at the mercy of a landlady, but in a *real home.*

Before, when I was out of work, I was lost. On one side, the landlady, hounding me for rent. On the other side, the terror of the street. Now I had even more than the protection of the Home.

I had a friend—Miss Simons. *An understanding* friend, with the power to help me. And back of it all, Mrs. Hellman.

Peeping into Miss Simons's office, I saw she was busy with the matron and secretary. Her head jerked with approving little nods, as she dictated her monthly report. "Every room in the house is filled. The long waiting list shows the far-reaching need of our institution.

"The moral and religious talks on Friday evening are doing much to give the girls that come to us a new outlook on life, a higher vision of their obligation to be patriotic and useful women.

"There has been a decided improvement in the moral and the social tone of the dancing, since Mrs. Moskowitz gave a very fascinating, illustrated talk on how dances are conducted uptown."

Miss Simons paused. Her forehead grooved into small, worried wrinkles under her smooth white hair.

"I feel strongly that a good report must be always optimistic in tone," she said, turning to the matron. "But what can I find to say encouraging about the Domestic Training course? In previous reports, I have been able to speak of the splendid new equipment, the up-to-date appliances, the efficiency of the new teacher. I can't play up these things again. And you know how Mrs. Hellman's heart is set on making a success of it."

"The fact is," broke in the matron, "out of the twelve girls we've been able to persuade to take the course, only seven remained."

By the way the frown deepened on Miss Simons's face, I felt like tiptoeing off. Now was not the time to tell her my troubles. But just then she looked up and saw me.

"What is it, Adele?" Miss Simons smiled.

"May I see you alone for a minute?"

She went with me into her inner office.

"Oh, Miss Simons, I—I—I—you know after the holiday rush—it gets slow in the stores. Mr. Bloomberg laid off three girls. And Miss Simons—I—"

"I'm sorry, Adele. Your board paid?"

"Yes—no—that is—I paid that first week—but last Monday—to-morrow will be two weeks—"

"Oh, dear! That is too bad. You know the rules. Two weeks is the time limit—with no exception."

I felt her eyes on me, cold, motionless.

"I don't want to discourage you, Adele, certainly. But our deficit for unpaid board last year was so appalling—and we have so many on our waiting list who can pay—"

Was this the friend to lean on in my need?

A horrible fear tightened my throat. That safe, sheltered feeling of having a *home* swept from under me. What was the beauty of this place—why this polite, kind, low voice when there was no heart to feel with me when I was down?

"Have you looked for work? What are your plans?"

"What *can* I do? I'd be willing to do anything—anything—"

Miss Simons seemed to be thinking hard, taking me in from under lowered lids. Then her face lighted up. "Why, Adele! I have just the opportunity for you! You must join our training school for domestic service."

"Domestic service!" Was I to be lost to myself as a servant? Come down from all I dreamed of being to washing dishes, peeling potatoes, taking orders from a mistress? Then the horrible days searching for work rushed over me. Getting up each day with lead in my feet, crushed with the sense that I had no place to go, no place where I could hang up my hat and coat. Driving myself all day, from store to store. Turned down. Unwanted. Yet rushing around hopelessly, *begging* to be wanted. Watching for the postman to bring some word from the ads I answered. Hurrying to offices hours ahead to be the first on the line only to see a shut door with the sign:

Positions Filled

That Fourteenth Street Bargain Store. Told to come at eight in the morning. Waiting with a mob of other girls till noon, only to have the man turn us all away for a girl who looked like a painted peacock. Morning gone. Hope gone. . . .

Employment agencies tearing out your insides with a million questions. Father. Mother. Religion. Experience. Always asking for experience. Questions I couldn't answer. Questions I wouldn't answer. . . . At the last place, they demanded fingerprints. I broke out: "I'm no criminal. I'm only looking for work. What do you want with fingerprints?" "Sorry. We employ only courteous people." . . .

"You shouldn't hesitate, Adele." Miss Simons's insistent voice kept on. "A moment ago you said you wanted to do anything. Can't you trust me to counsel you for your good?"

I—a servant? Even in our worst poverty in Poland none of our people had ever been servants. Tailors, storekeepers, but never a servant. Should I be the first to go down?

"You see, my dear, you're just the kind of a girl I like to help *on*. And this course is a real chance for you. Trained domestics have work the whole year round. Better living conditions, better chance to save money than any other class of workers. Just now, while you're out of work, take advantage of this splendid training."

"Thank you, Miss Simons. I guess you know what's best."

37

"I think I do know what's best for you." Miss Simons put an encouraging hand on my shoulder. "But you solved your own problem and made me proud of you."

Somehow, her smile, her praise left me more lonely than ever before. I was going into something that was not me.

"There's no reason why we should lose any time. Come along. I'll introduce you to the teacher."

The huge, white, glittering kitchen was almost empty. In the far corner, a few girls in blue print dresses with large white aprons were bending over their stoves. So pretty and businesslike. Nora O'Flaherty looked up." "Gawd! The ould girl got another recruit! Welcome to the bloody ranks!"

Miss Perkins, the teacher, tall, thin, in her white, starched uniform, reminded me of the head doctor in a hospital. She buzzed with importance as she assigned me to a stove, a locker, and a uniform.

Now began the worry how to break the news to my room-mates. It had to come out. There was the uniform.

When I put it on, Minnie and Sadie stared at me—speechless. Then they began making little clicking sounds between their tongue and teeth. "You—you—a servant?"

"A fine chance you'll have to get a man, if you can only invite him through the kitchen door."

"They couldn't make me into a servant for a million dollars. Once a servant, always a servant."

Very slowly, I buttoned my apron, the badge of the servant. I knew Minnie and Sadie and all the other girls who worked in shops and factories would stop associating with me. I had dropped out of their class.

Suddenly, I raised my chin, high over their heads. "I'm not begging. I'm not asking charity. Honest work. Work that has to be done. If housework can't lift me, I'll lift housework. I'll fight for the right of servant girls to receive their boy friends in the parlour. I'll do for servants what Florence Nightingale did for nurses."

"Miss Simons's pet!" they sneered. "Anything that old dame says she eats up alive."

"I'll show you in America *all work is respectable*. In America, dish-washers and hod-carriers can also be citizens with the same rights as the President."

I stalked out of the room, lifted into greater strength by their scornful laughter.

The class began with inspection. Miss Perkins, stiff and straight like a drill sergeant, sang out: "Hands up!"

"Put them up, kid!" My Irish friend nudged me. "It's a stick-up. The ould bandit may shoot you."

I threw up my hands.

"Let me see your nails," commanded Miss Perkins.

I turned my hands over.

"You must scrub them with a nail brush. You can't touch food here unless your hands are absolutely immaculate."

Her critical eye peered closer at me. "Your hair needs brushing. A hair net under your cap will make it neater."

"But hair nets are so ugly."

Miss Perkins drew her lips thinly together. "This is no beauty parlour."

The inspection dropped to my shoes. "Shoes must be shined every day. If you wish to be a professional, every detail of your appearance must be perfect."

39

"Sure! Spit on them, but make them shine," Nora laughed.

In front of me were all kinds of dirty dishes from the morning's breakfast.

"Sort your dishes," commanded Miss Perkins.

"What's that?" I asked.

"Look in your notebook, rule one."

"All the dishes together, it's so much quicker."

A steely glint appeared in Miss Perkins's eye. But her voice was low and ladylike. "Are you trying to teach me how they wash dishes on the East Side? You are here to learn how to work scientifically."

I thought I'd die of dullness trying to be "scientific." A whole morning spent on different ways to make white sauce.

This learning to be a cook—what did it mean? Did I really want to spend every day of my life on nothing more important than cooking things that you eat up anyway?

And while I was trying to think it out, my soup burned, my milk boiled over, dishes dropped from my hands. Still I kept on, trying to force myself into an interest in what I was doing.

And then, when Miss Simons visited the class, I heard Miss Perkins say: "Absolutely hopeless. She seems to be dreaming half the time."

My cheeks blazed with shame. My throat clutched with the hurt of it. I had forced myself to be a cook to please Miss Simons. And yet I had not brains enough for that!

"Never mind, darlin'," Nora's arms were around me, "many an ould cat got the slip from a wee little mouse. We'll fool the ould girl yet. Don't worry."

But I did worry.

That night, when everybody was in bed, sound asleep, I alone was fiercely awake. I turned from side to side, trying to close my eyes, but it kept going round and round in my head: "She's hopeless! Absolutely hopeless!"

I jumped out of bed, flung on my kimono, stole through the halls, down the stairs into the huge, dark, empty kitchen. My fingers found the electric switch. The place leaped into light.

It was just before the weekly cleaning. Miss Perkins had had a class for the women of the neighbourhood that very evening, and it was our duty to clean up after them the following morning.

I set myself to scour the tables, the stoves. When they were perfect, I polished the huge kitchen range. Next I got a pail of hot soapsuds and scrubbed the floor. Until the gray light of morning crept through the windows I worked. I should have been exhausted, but I did not even feel tired.

Within me was a sense of wings released. I felt that no matter how the other girls looked down on me, I had proved myself to myself. I knew now that I could put such heart and soul into cooking and cleaning, even if I had to be a servant, I would not be a low-down servant.

When I entered the classroom after breakfast, Miss Perkins and the girls were in a state of wondering excitement.

"What has happened to this kitchen?" asked Miss Perkins. "Who's done this work overnight?"

"I did." I looked straight into Miss Perkins's eye. "I wanted to show you."

Miss Simons was sent for. With pride, Miss Perkins pointed to my work. "After all, my training does bear fruit. When I take a girl in hand, no matter how hopeless she is at the beginning, in the end she goes my way."

Later that morning, just as I put the bread in the oven, Miss

Simons came in with the Board of Directors. She whispered something to Miss Perkins, who turned to me. "Ruth will take care of your bread. Brush the flour off your elbow, pull your cap a little straighter. The ladies wish to speak to you."

So there—with Miss Simons on my right hand, Miss Perkins on my left, I was led to meet Mrs. Hellman and the other ladies.

They crowded around and beamed on me:

"We're so proud of you, my dear!"

"If we could only bring this kitchen to the tenements!"

"God help the tenement!" whispered Nora, while buttoning my apron.

Suddenly, I loved the work I had hated. I felt that nothing on earth could keep me down. There was a fire inside of me that could cook and clean its way into the hearts of people just as if I were an actress on the stage.

I had to pour out my gratitude in a letter to the ladies. I had to make them feel what I felt or die. I worked on my composition the whole night. When I had finished, I read it aloud to myself with such deep feeling that tears came to my eyes.

Ladies of the Working Girls' Home! Benefactors of Humanity! Saviours of My Soul!

A wanderer was once crossing the desert. He was tired and hungry. The sun shed its hot rays upon him and his lips were parched with thirst. All at once he came upon a beautiful oasis, trees laden with fruit to appease his hunger and a cooling stream of water to quench his thirst. After he had eaten the fruit and drunk of the water, he was thinking in his heart prayerfully, "O cooling water, O God-sent fruit! I would have perished without you. What can I give you of myself in return except my heart-

42

deep wishes that you go on saving other lives as you saved mine?"

I thought the world was a desert of landladies. I was so tired and hungry and thirsty for a little bit of human kindness. And suddenly, in the depths of this heartless city, I came upon this oasis, this Beautiful Home for Working Girls that saved my life. I have no words deep enough to thank you with, I can only say dumbly over and over again, Benefactors of Humanity! Saviours of my Soul! May you go on saving other girls as you have saved me. May the Home be a lighthouse of love to all the homeless ones of the world.

With everlasting gratitude and burning appreciation out of a full heart.

Forever and always thankfully yours,

Adele Lindner.

I took the letter to Miss Simons. Breathlessly, I watched her read it. I couldn't judge from her expression how she liked it. Then my heart jumped in my throat with pleasure when Miss Simons said: "It makes me happy, indeed, Adele, that you feel as you do about the Home. It's a great satisfaction to me that my advice to you has been justified. I shall keep your letter to read at our Board meeting. We may even decide to include it in our next year's catalogue."

She put her hand over my shoulder. "My dear, I see a great future for you. I shall make it a point to see that you are sent to Training School."

Chapter Five

Within a few days, I received a note from Mrs. Hellman!

My dear Adele:

At the last meeting of the Board of Directors, Miss Simons read us your letter. We were so touched by it that we decided you deserve an opportunity to fit yourself to serve in a large way. My dear! We are going to send you to a Training School!

I feel sure you will prove worthy of our faith in you. It is only through people of your type that we can hope to spread our message.

Will you kindly call at my house at ten o'clock Monday morning to talk over our plans for your education?

I have also some clothes for you which I think might do very nicely for your new work.

Cordially yours,
Sarah S. Hellman.

I felt like a heroine in a story book. A movie in real life.

All the way up to the Hellman house, Training School was forgotten. Back of all my whirling brain was one thought: I am going to *his* house. Will I see him? What will he say to me? What will I say to him?

In my high-flying, romantic mood, I not only imagined myself in love with *him,* I even saw *him in love with me.*

I saw clearer than sight his tall, straight body. The aristocratic face. The soft gray eyes with the curious light in them that kept me guessing what he was feeling, what he was thinking. The way his smile lingered. The calmness filling the air around him. The very aloofness fascinated me.

Pushing the doorbell had for me the thrill of adventure.

"I want to see Mrs. Hellman," I said, smiling gaily at the butler.

He didn't seem to notice my smile at all. He just said, in a cold voice, "Does Mrs. Hellman expect you?"

"Yes, she does. I'm Adele Lindner."

As he stood there, hesitating, I caught sight of Arthur Hellman, coming downstairs, whistling to himself.

A whirl of colours blinded my eyes.

I wanted to speak to him, but my lips seemed stuck together.

Then he saw me. "Are you waiting for Mother?" he said, with a smile of recognition. "She'll be down in a moment." He bowed and went out.

He remembered me! I could feel he liked me. I couldn't breathe for happiness.

"This way, please." The butler led me to the reception room. "Mrs. Hellman is coming directly."

For the first time, I saw the inside of the other world. What rugs, statues, paintings! Only in windows on Fifth Avenue had I seen these things of art. I touched the fringe of a Persian hanging.

The cool smoothness of a green vase. Hothouse roses. Orchids. How much finer, more sensitive the Hellmans must be than plain people—they with so much beauty around them every day of their lives.

"Good-morning, Adele." Mrs. Hellman came toward me smiling. "What can I do for you?—oh, of course—I remember. I wrote and asked you to come so that we might talk over our plans for your training."

She took my hand and held it. "First I want to thank you for your lovely letter. It is a great happiness to find a girl who really appreciates all we try to do for her. It is my hope that this training in domestic science will enable you to become a leader among your people. You can teach them that the joy of living consists in serving others."

I couldn't speak. My eyes on her eyes. My dumb lips drinking inspiration out of her lips.

"It is almost a religion with me, this mission of teaching the masses that there is no such thing as drudgery. There are no menial tasks if you bring to your work the spirit of service and the love of honest toil. . . ."

I just kept looking at her, while her beautiful thoughts, one after another, fed my heart like poems.

"If only women could bring into their homes this self-sacrificing attitude toward life! Isn't it just as satisfying to the soul to feel you have scrubbed a floor faithfully as to be mistress of the house? In doing your cheerful, conscientious best, in your humble sphere, you are doing your part toward the harmony and perfection of the whole universe."

She rose, still smiling. "Now, my dear, about the clothes. I told Marie to have the parcel ready for you."

46

She rang for the maid to give me the package.

"I hope it won't be too heavy for you to carry."

"Too heavy? Oh, no. May I look at the things? I'm so crazy for pretty clothes."

Mrs. Hellman glanced at me, seemed to hesitate. But only for a moment. Then in her low voice she told the maid to show me to a room upstairs.

Breathlessly, I tore open the package. An afternoon dress, a party dress, silk stockings with little holes, linen collars slightly frayed, a sweater a little worn at the sleeves. But one thing was almost new—a brown sport suit with a hat to match, just the thing that I would have chosen for myself if I ever had the money. In a moment, I slipped it on. It fitted perfectly. I was so thrilled with the elegance of my appearance, I rushed down with open arms to Mrs. Hellman.

"See what you've done for me!" I threw my arms around her and kissed her. Suddenly, I became aware of the cold way she turned her cheek to me. There was a silent moment of strain. My arms dropped.

"Thank you so much! Now I've taken enough of your time." I started to go.

In the mirror, I saw Mrs. Hellman make a swift little motion to her cheek. She was wiping with her tiny handkerchief the spot I had kissed.

I felt as if a piece of ice had dropped into my blood. My hands turned cold. My heart cold. But within, every nerve was burning.

"Just a moment, Adele." Mrs. Hellman reached out her arm, graciously drew me to a chair beside her.

"Let me tell you what I propose to do for you. The Board of Directors are paying for your tuition, and I want to help you with

47

your other expenses. But you must be very careful and systematic. To begin with, write out a list of everything you're quite sure you cannot do without. If I think you need all the things you put down, I'll advance you the money."

"Thank you. Thank you," I smiled miserably. "You're so kind."

"We will consider it a loan. And some day, when you're able, you can return it to me, or send some other girl to Training School."

Again my lips mumbled thanks.

Out in the street, the package of clothes turned to lead in my hands. I caught glimpses of myself in the mirror of a passing shop window. A worried stare lurked in my eyes. Though I had on a more becoming hat and suit than I had ever worn in my life, yet I could not hold my head as high as before.

When I got back to the Home, a new girl sat beside Miss Simons's desk. The card index of files out. Miss Simons writing down her history as she had written mine. That new girl's face was shining as mine had shone when I first came here. It seemed so long ago. I felt a thousand years older now.

A cleaning woman scrubbing the front hall left a curious smell of disinfectant that I had never noticed before.

Upstairs, passing through the corridors, I saw, for the first time, all the rooms alike. The same beds, tables, and chairs, set in the same places, as if the rooms and everything in them were turned out by a machine.

I shut the door. Sat down to write the list for Mrs. Hellman. But her words kept drilling into my ears. *"If I think you need the things you put down, I'll advance you the money."*

The pencil dropped from my hand. I picked up the last book

Shlomoh had sent me. Thoughts all mixed together crowded up in me. Suddenly, I hurled the book at the mirror. It opened at the title page, "The Insulted and the Injured." Over the printed words rose Mrs. Hellman. That cold cheek. The little hidden gesture in the mirror.

A wild thought came to me. I wanted to take the clothes back to Mrs. Hellman and tell her: "I'm nothing and nobody in your eyes. I'm only one of your damn charities. Why fool myself?"

I jammed the things together, still talking to myself: "I've lived till now without kind rich ladies to help me. I can go on living without them. I'll go back where I came from." I sank down limply over the bundle of clothes. Go back? Where? To whom? My landlady—when I'm out of work? Go back, when hundreds and thousands are walking the streets idle?

What will Mrs. Hershbein and Shlomoh think of me when they see my grand plans to rise in the world turned to nothing?

I can't go back. I've got to go on. Even if it kills me, I've got to go on.

With tight lips, I wrote out the list of expenses for Mrs. Hellman. Just as I had once hardened myself to cauterize a blood-poisoned finger in the flame, so I hardened myself to meet the friendly kindness of my benefactress.

As I sat again in the reception room, waiting for Mrs. Hellman, I looked around with cold eyes at the things that had inspired me the day before.

The flowers, the rugs—the room itself had lost its magic, its beauty. Through everything I saw the cold way Mrs. Hellman had drawn back when I rushed to kiss her. Why should they have the glory of giving and we the shame of taking like beggars the bare necessities of life?

49

"What can I do for you, Adele?" Mrs. Hellman came toward me smiling her kindest smile.

"What can I do for *you*?" I longed to hurl back at her.

The first time Mrs. Hellman had greeted me with *"What-can-I-do-for-you?"* I had felt only her warm friendliness. But now, this professional *"What-can-I-do-for-you?"* hit me like a slap in the face.

Avoiding her eyes, I said: "Don't you remember you told me to write out a list of things I needed?"

"Oh, yes. Let me see it."

Mrs. Hellman scanned through the items.

Coat for winter	$25.00
Shoes	10.00
Warm gloves	1.50
Four pairs silk stockings	5.00
Carfare and incidentals for one month	6.00

"That totals up to forty-seven dollars and fifty cents. That isn't a bit bad, Adele. But I think we can even save on that."

"Save?" I threw back my shoulders and sat up very straight.

"The coat," Mrs. Hellman went on. "My daughter, Edna, just bought two new ones that she really doesn't need. She has several in perfectly good condition, and I'm sure we can find one that will do for you. That item is off our list," and Mrs. Hellman put a line through the twenty-five dollars.

"Now, as for shoes. I think Macy's are having a sale of sensible college shoes with broad toes and low heels for seven forty-nine. That's a dollar and a half saved. . . .

"Stockings? Didn't Marie put in quite a few pairs in your package?"

"Yes. But they were full of holes."

50

"Don't they teach you how to darn and mend?"

I reddened but said nothing.

"Well, the ones I gave you were silk and really only suitable for evening wear. You will need about two pairs of warm ones. And cotton stockings are so much more practical and durable than silk. I think, if you fix up the others I gave you, you will have quite enough. . . .

"Carfare and incidentals? Let me see. You have about twenty school days. That amounts to two dollars. What do you want with the other four?"

"I counted something for pencils and stationery. And I don't know, but I felt—I would have to have a little money for extras."

Mrs. Hellman made no further comment. She did a little figuring on the margin of the paper. When she looked up again, the momentary irritation that had been on her face was gone. She said enthusiastically, "See how much we've been able to cut down by just a little knowledge and management! Remember, my dear, it's a wise old saying, 'a penny saved is a penny earned.' Some day, you'll realize that your greatest blessing in life is the discipline of being poor and having to count your pennies." — but what does she know about being poor

"Thank you! Thank you, for all your trouble."

But out in the street, I stood still. Stunned. Seeing nothing.

"God! What's happening to me? I hate myself. I hate her for helping me! And I hate myself for taking her help!"

51

Chapter Six

I opened the door of my room. The afternoon sunshine flooded in. I stepped over to the window, felt the freshness of the white curtains, the red and green geraniums. The lovely quiet of the clean, wide street. I thought of the dark hole in the wall at Mrs. Greenberg's. In that whole block of tenements there wasn't as much air as in this one room. . . . This view is all yours. This sun, this sky, this life-giving air—yours. Beggar! Stop whining poverty! . . . *should be thankful of what she has*

I stretched out on my bed, let the healing sunshine pour in, wash away the mean little hurts that shut me out from all the beauty around me. . . . What things you have to be thankful for! Mrs. Hellman! She might have spent her time playing cards, and stuffing herself like those fat women on Riverside Drive. Instead, she built this Home, works from morning till night trying to do good! . . . I saw Mrs. Hellman step out of the velvet comforts of her luxurious home, go down into the dirt and noise where poor people live, to create this Home. . . .

How wonderful it must be to live for others!

The more I thought of her, the more I realized what an ingrate I was. I saw myself one of those "gimme-gimme" girls. Give them a finger and they want your whole hand. . . .

The worst thing about being poor—thinking always of yourself. As Mrs. Hellman steps out of her riches to do so much for us, why can't one of us step out of her poverty to do some little thing for her?

My heart rushed to Mrs. Hellman. I loved her the more because for a moment I had been disloyal to her in my thoughts. With a new sense of gratitude, I hurried down to the telephone booth to call her up.

As I picked up the receiver, I glanced at the clock. Perhaps this was not the time to bother her. Perhaps I ought to wait till morning, when she attends to the business of the Home. But this isn't business. I can't wait! I can't breathe till I tell her all. I want to give her my heart—my appreciation of her. . . .

The butler answered the telephone. "May I take your message?"

"Oh, no. I must speak to Mrs. Hellman herself."

"She is busy with guests for dinner. Is it important?"

"Of course it's important. Please tell her it's Adele."

Mrs. Hellman came to the 'phone. "Well-l—?"

Something, so impatient in the tone of her voice, froze all my thoughts. I could only stutter: "I—I—Mrs. Hellman—I—"

"Well?" with rising annoyance. *What can I do for you?*

"Oh—I—nothing I want you to do for me.—I just wanted—I— you're such a real friend—I thought, maybe—oh, if I could only tell you all I feel—"

"My dear! It's very awkward to be called away at this hour. Has anything happened?"

"Oh, no. Nothing happened. I just wanted to—"

"But can't it wait till to-morrow, Adele?"

"Please—Mrs. Hellman—"

"But, Adele, I'm with my family now."

"Oh, Mrs. Hellman—"

"I've done all I could for you, and will always do all I can, but, my dear, you must never call me on the 'phone." *doesn't want any association besides helping*

"I'm sorry—I—"

While I was still talking, the receiver clicked at the other end. Then the voice of the telephone operator: "Number, please."

Through the shame that stung through every nerve of me, I almost began to see the funny side of it all. I began to laugh at myself, at Mrs. Hellman, but it was hard, mirthless laughter. . . . *The saviour of humanity* off her guard! And you—object of charity! Because she was kind enough to throw down to you her old clothes and send you to the Training School for Servants—how dare you forget yourself? How dare you voice even your gratitude out of turn? . . .

Chapter Seven

That night, tossing from side to side, restlessly crumpling my pillow, torn by the little worries swarming in the dark—it suddenly came to me. There is a way out of the Home. From Mrs. Hellman, doling out the nickels with uplifting words, from the whole sickening farce of Big Sistering the Working Girl and What-can-I-do-for-you-my-dear. Shlomoh Hershbein. He loves me. . . . And I like him—well enough. He has his teacher's job now. He's the way out from all my troubles.

But Arthur Hellman! Give up dreaming of him? Like giving up the light, the air to keep alive. Giving up "a sky for a ceiling."

What's the beauty of the sky when you've no roof over your head? Shall I let longing—a hope—a dream keep me from the shelter that Shlomoh could give me? Love? Another luxury denied to the poor. If you must have love and are poor—read about it in novels. Dream about it at night. By day, you have to buy bread and pay rent. Marry Shlomoh—you can still have your dreams of Arthur Hellman.

I invited Shlomoh to come the following evening. My letter was more than kind. It was meant to be. The next morning I received such a gushing response, I could barely read it through.

Dear Love of Life! Adele, My Heart's Friend!

I hope you are as happy as I am this glorious morning. Heaven opened in my heart with that letter from you. Just the sight of your precious handwriting stirred up in me such a tumult of emotion, I walked the streets my hand touching the dear envelope your hand had touched. I forgot time, work, everything was swept away in the glorious image of you—you only.

I feel it one of the settled facts of the universe that we are for each other as the sun is for the earth. You and I—with the great books of the world—can heaven hold more?

O ineffably radiant woman! O everything ravishingly contradictory—O woman many-sided as life who blesses like life and wounds like life. Adorable one! How can I breathe till I see you.

I tore the letter into shreds. Why wasn't he a man like Arthur Hellman? I wanted to call back my invitation—never see him again. Too late.

I found him waiting for me in the reception room. His face almost hidden by a huge bunch of roses clasped tightly in his arms. As I entered, he leaped up, stumbling toward me, shoving the flowers against my cheek. He jerked out his hand to grasp mine. What a hand! The damp skin clinging to my fingers felt like a limp fish wriggling against my palm. Not to hurt his feelings, I twisted my mouth into a smile.

"Oh, Shlomoh! You shouldn't have spent all that money. But these roses are so lovely."

"You are more lovely than all the roses in all the gardens of the world."

He kept mopping the perspiration trickling down his face, casting shy, self-conscious glances at me.

I busied myself arranging the flowers in a vase, to delay for another moment sitting down beside him to make conversation.

Funny, clumsy old Shlomoh in his new suit. Sleeves too short, collar so big it wrinkled up the back of his neck. His hands fidgeting nervously with his necktie. Once I had told him his tie was too broad and shapeless. Now it was too stiff and narrow. And such a shade of green!

"You look like a model in a show window," I laughed. "New from head to foot. The movies ought to get after you."

He did not hear a word, staring at me with starved eyes.

The silence grew loud with his dumb pleading. His helplessness, his confusion, the famine crying out of his heart—the famine that I knew so well—and I—looking on, cold, aloof—like a Mrs. Hellman. Suddenly, I wanted to reach out to him with a warmth of understanding. But that hand! His touch turned me to ice.

I began to talk fast to hide the way I felt.

"How is your mother, Shlomoh? She must be terribly proud with her son a teacher in high school. I'll bet it's still the talk of the block. The neighbours must be still crowing around her, envying and congratulating."

"You should have seen her when she moved out of the janitor's flat to the front part of the house! It was the first thing we did when I got my position. No more janitor's work for her. Thank heaven. This morning I left her all excited fixing up her new kitchen with oilcloth and lace curtains just like a parlour. You're coming to our *Purim* feast, of course? We even got a new chair—specially for you."

"I'm afraid I can't come."

57

"Oh, but you must come—Mother's expecting you."

"I'm not in the mood for visiting now." *[handwritten: something snobbish]*

He leaned forward, his self-consciousness forgotten in his concern for me. "You do look tired. What's happened?"

"How can I begin to tell you?"

"You must tell me, Adele! What am I here for? Don't you feel you can count on me for anything?—Me—your friend.—And I thought you were so happy here."

"If I were to tell what's giving me the jim-jams, you'd think me crazy." I laughed loud out of sheer misery. "Think of two hundred girls eating the same hash out of the same thick plates, at the same time, every Monday and Thursday, week in and week out. Such things get me so nervous I could scream. But it isn't just the hash. It's this mortgage on my soul I've given them for letting me live here, for sending me to Training School."

[handwritten margin note: regretting ex.. / there? / charity / dine "devil"(?)]

"If I could in the least little way be of use to you, it would make me so happy. What wouldn't I do—if you would only let me. Oh, Adele, won't you let me take you away?"

There was something so loyal in his eyes. It was a loyalty I could lean on. Where could I find a better friend? Impulsively, I reached out to him.

He seized my hand. Before I knew it, he kissed my fingers. Hungrily. Ravenously. Wet lips against my skin. Devouring lips that would eat me up if I let them. I broke away, fled to the window. "Let me alone—oh, let me alone!" I could have screamed.

"Adele! Forgive me."

I couldn't look at him.

His hurt eyes began their silent pleading again. He picked up a book, staring at it unseeingly, fingered the pages, threw it down. Then, turning to me humbly:

"How could I dream that God would be so good to me—that you would love me? I'm mad. Forgive me."

"There's nothing to forgive, Shlomoh. I like you. You're a good friend—but—but—"

He shook his head dejectedly. His lips opened to speak. But no words came. His eyes hurt me—and I was helpless. Slowly, he picked up his hat. Gave me one look and walked out.

For a long time I sat without moving, without hearing a thing. I became dimly aware of rain outside. It was blowing furiously. I closed the window, slumped back into the chair.

Poor Shlomoh! Why can't I feel for you when you're around as I do when you're away? . . . No. No. Marrying you to save myself, I'd sink lower than eating dust at their hands. . . . After all, how long will my slavery last? Just another year. Then I'll be free and independent. . . . No, Shlomoh. I respect you too much. I like you too much. . . .

And then I was suddenly startled. Shlomoh, fumbling with his hat, stood before me. "It's raining—I—I had to come back—for a nickel—for carfare."

His new suit was drenched. The green of his necktie dripped over his white shirt.

"I—I—gave all my money to the florist," he blurted. "I—forgot—I had no change."

Schlemiel!

Chapter Eight

As time went on, I became aware of two people in me. One Adele, cringing, truckling—to get on. The other, watching her own funeral—cold, critical.

On my way to Mrs. Hellman, I did not see the streets nor the people passing by. Lost in the muddle of my mind. . . . What's become of you? Hanger-on! You've ceased to believe in yourself. Glad to get even the crumbs that fall from the master's table.

. . . Well, I've got to get on! Most people don't even know when they're deceiving themselves. That poor student in *Crime and Punishment.* , at least finds what Chlomin gives her

I laughed out loud. . . . He reasoned himself into becoming a murderer. You reasoned yourself into becoming a flunkey. Going to *her* house, week in and week out, as a servile, grateful little Working Girl, making believe she's saving your soul. . . .

. . . Poor Mrs. Hellman! Forever being done by the beggars crying for help! . . . That actress. How she came fawning, wheedling, begging Mrs. Hellman to save her life with a hundred-dollar loan. As soon as she landed a job—no more use for Mrs. Hellman. . . .

. . . Maybe being rich isn't all sunshine and roses. What do I know of the troubles of Mrs. Hellman? With all her beauty treatments, her Paris gowns, she can't keep her husband's love. I and all the other wretches who eat out of her hand are ready to pounce on her—bite the hand that feeds us. The horrible ingratitude of the poor! We're all down on the Mrs. Hellmans for having what we want. For once, I felt so sorry for Mrs. Hellman, I forgot the shame I had always experienced going through the servants' entrance.

I had been taking the waitress's place on her day off, ever since I began the Teacher's Course in Domestic Science. Mrs. Hellman had suggested in that way I could get some good first-hand experience "observing how a household of the first class arranged the details of its service."

Her face had beamed with the pleasure of doing good. Her hand had rested on my shoulder, as she explained: "I have to pay someone from the agency for this work, Adele. You might just as well have the money. You know how strongly I believe the best way for us to help our girls is to provide opportunity for them to help themselves."

I needed every cent I could possibly earn; but more than the money was the chance to watch the Hellman world. To listen to their talk was as exciting as going to a play.

As I placed the silver, I heard voices from the other room. The Board of Directors of the Home. They had met that morning at Mrs. Hellman's house for their regular monthly session.

I paused in the setting of the table, peered through the crack in the dining-room door.

Snooping? But it was my only way to learn what was going on in the other world.

Noiselessly, I pushed the door slightly open. Straining to see them all. Alert to catch every word.

Mrs. Stone's chair creaked as she raised her two hundred pounds, gowned in chiffon velvet. "I think we're weakening the moral fibre of our girls—doing them a positive injury with so much pampering."

With her jewelled hand she patted back the carefully arranged marcel over her ear. "I'm taking a course in Social Welfare with Dean Sopwell. Only yesterday he told us how struggle and hardship strengthen character. I've been quite worried about the future of our girls. Are we using all our knowledge and wisdom to help them face life? Face the conditions in which they are born and to which they must adjust themselves? You all know the besetting vices of the working class are discontent and love of pleasure. Have we the right to give our girls luxuries they can't afford when they're out of our care?"

"The Home was created to give them a higher standard of living," said Mrs. Hellman. "All those things denied them in their cruel poverty."

"But, Mrs. Hellman! Fond as we are of our girls, we must not let our affection for them cloud our vision as to what is wisest and best for their future welfare."

"I agree with you, Mrs. Stone," came from Mrs. Gordon. "We must not confuse their standards of living with our own."

"Yes. Yes. It would be utterly disastrous for them to get wrong notions of superiority," added Mrs. White.

Mrs. Stone smiled, and continued: "We must bear in mind our girls come from the working class and will marry among their own kind. The corner stone of their character and happiness should be a love of honest toil and a devotion to thrift and economy. It is our first duty to teach them that a penny saved is a penny earned."

I saw them nod approvingly, one to the other.

"The way they dress these days! Ridiculous! Shop girls wearing silk stockings, fur coats. Where's it all leading to?"

Mrs. Gordon smoothed her broad-tail bag that matched her made-to-order broad-tail shoes. "If we could only make them see how much better simple things are than all their finery."

"Remember these poor girls won't have us forever." Mrs. Hellman's voice was warm with pity. "We must give them all we possibly can while they're with us, so the Home will be the happiest memory of their lives."

"Yes. Yes. There's something in that," echoed Mrs. White. "How will they ever get on when we're no longer back of them?"

"Ladies, all this philosophizing is away from the main point. We've come to discuss the deficit in the Home's budget. We have certain funds to spend for the welfare of our girls, and we're not dispensing them with the greatest efficiency. Am I not right?"

I knew well the preacher of efficiency, Mrs. Gessenheim, the chairman of the Board. Everything about her spoke efficiency. Her snug-fitting toque, her tight lipsticked mouth, her navy-blue tailored dress, so elegantly perfect.

She picked up the treasurer's report, looked at it through her glasses. "We must call a halt somewhere. Our deficit is growing bigger each month. We must not only feed our girls within the limits of our income, but save enough for emergencies."

"Yes. Yes," murmured Mrs. White, in her soft, chiming-in voice. "There's something in that."

"We have no right to forget we're feeding an institution and not our own families."

Mrs. Gessenheim paused, looked about to see how effectively she had made her point. Then she went on in her positive tone:

"You all know the case of the Laura Sinclair Home. Mrs. Clark, the last superintendent, a nice, motherly soul and all that. But she wanted to give the girls food beyond the budget. And they got so heavily in debt, they had to close down."

"Of course they did," puffed Mrs. Stone, her cheeks mottling with indignation. "She tried to run the place without rules. Allowed the girls to come in all hours of the night. In no time the place got a bad name."

"Now they've come to me to solve their difficulties," Mrs. Gessenheim declared, triumphantly. "I told them at the first conference, if they want to keep within their budget, they must realize that an institution is an institution."

The murmur of assent grew into a loud chatter.

"All the Y. W. Homes are run on a strictly business basis. They don't allow their sympathies to overrule their better judgment."

"That's why they're so successful."

"After all, we're living in a commercial age."

"We ought to conduct the business of the Home the way an efficiency expert runs a factory. Now as my husband explained to me. . . ."

They all looked at her with reverent attention. The Gessenheim millions talked.

"In our smelting concern they use every by-product for profit. They melt junk to make pig iron. What's left over is turned into paper. You see, nothing is wasted in a successful business. Why not apply this efficiency to the Home?

"They don't need to have roast beef every Sunday. Why not buy the cheaper cuts? They're just as nourishing. Think of the saving if we give them chopped meat instead of roast beef."

Mrs. Hellman stood up, faced Mrs. Gessenheim with that in-

64

spired, missionary look that lighted up her eyes when she talked for the poor. "I think we ought to feed our girls even better than we do and find some other way to meet the deficit. You will all agree that good health is the most important thing for a working girl. I suggest that we do not economize in their diet."

"Yes. Yes. You're right, Mrs. Hellman," agreed Mrs. White. "Hungry people are always discontented."

"Nobody can say that the girls in our institution go hungry. There's always plenty to eat. But roast beef is only for people who can afford it." With this clinching remark, Mrs. Stone folded her jewelled hands.

"It's my birthday next Sunday," continued Mrs. Hellman. "I want to share my happiness by celebrating with the girls. Before this ruling goes into effect, I intend to give them a real treat—chicken, salad, ice cream, and cake."

Miss Simons fidgeted unhappily. A troubled shadow flickered in her pale blue eyes. "It's very sweet of you to want to make the girls happy for a day, Mrs. Hellman. But we must beware of rousing their appetites. It will only lead to greater discontent later on."

"Discontent? Ridiculous!" sniffed Mrs. Gessenheim.

Miss Simons raised her thin eyebrows, tightened her lips. "It's very hard to keep the undisciplined girls who come to us from wanting more and more. I had a case. Minnie Rosen wanted to spend ten dollars out of her twelve-dollar wages for a permanent wave. Because she's just engaged—as she puts it, 'crazy about her man.'"

And so, for the good of the girls' souls Mrs. Hellman's wish to feast them was overruled.

"It would have made such a splendid newspaper story," murmured Mrs. Hellman. "Two hundred poor girls made happy because of my birthday. And publicity for the Home is so essential."

"Speaking of publicity," broke in Mrs. Stone. "Isn't the Press sending camera men to take our pictures to-day?"

"My secretary phoned. They ought to be here by now."

"The *Tribune* and *Times* have made so little response. They don't seem to realize the tremendous importance of our work. Isn't it amazing—these papers search everywhere for news and turn deaf ears to the Betterment of the Working Girl."

"Editors seem to forget the poor except the Hundred Neediest Cases at Christmas. The burden falls on us three hundred and sixty-five days in the year—"

"We need a news story with a clever touch that will turn the public eye to our cause. Something should be published each week showing the wonderful work we're carrying on, to prepare the public for our drive next fall."

"I know a reporter on the *News*," Mrs. White spoke up. "I'll invite her to lunch. She'll do anything for me."

"The tabloids are easy enough to handle. They're crazy to get pictures of important people. I have an idea how we can get in better touch with the editors of the *Tribune,* the *Times,* the *World.* Let's ask their wives to tea. . . . Mrs. Hellman, couldn't you arrange a special affair one day next week, invite a few celebrities as an excuse to get them?"

"I suppose it's my duty. Anything for our cause. The responsibility of our position makes it necessary to make so many sacrifices and concessions, but I'm always *so glad* to do my part."

Mrs. Hellman arose, glanced at her watch, and went to the phone.

66

I heard fragments of her telephone conversation:

"This is Mrs. Hellman speaking. *The* Mrs. *Morris* Hellman. President of the Federation of Charities, Director of Working Girls' Associations. . . . The photographers have not yet arrived. The delay is embarrassing. Please see that they're sent immediately. It's most important that our photographs and the article be featured in this Sunday's supplement as planned."

She hung up, turned to her guests and sighed. "It seems we'll have to wait till after lunch for our pictures. The editor—poor man! No sense of values! Why, he was about to send his entire staff of photographers to that stupid financial delegation from Europe. Fortunately, I called up in time."

The meeting was adjourned. I brought in the cocktails; announced, "Luncheon served."

They seated themselves about the flower-bedecked table, shining with silver and rare Venetian glass.

Mrs. Stone, swallowing a mouthful of almonds, led the conversation: "I shall expect you all to come to the bridge party next Wednesday. Remember the money goes to my orphans."

"Your orphans?" asked Mrs. Gordon suggestively.

For answer, Mrs. Stone took a carefully folded paper out of her purse. "Shall I read you what they wrote me?" With a childlike, happy smile, she ended the letter: "For your magnificent donation, your name will be written in letters of gold on the tables of our institution."

"Isn't it nice of them to memorialize your good deeds while you're still alive?" purred Miss Simons.

"I've always said the best pleasure you can buy for your money is to help the poor."

67

"It's a pleasure to help, if they are grateful," said Mrs. Gordon. "But haven't you noticed, my dear, in so many cases, the more you do for people the less they appreciate it?"

"That's why I'm taking this course with Dean Sopwell, so as to know how to help wisely. We who set out to serve humanity must cultivate a scientific attitude of mind. After all, we're living in a scientific age; and even social work must be done scientifically."

"Speaking of science," chirped Mrs. White. "My *masseuse* has just returned from Sweden. She brought back perfectly wonderful new reducing exercises. Think of it! I lost a pound last week." And she smoothed down her over-rounded bosom hopefully. "There's no excuse nowadays for any woman losing her youthful figure."

"But it's so tiresome, not to be able to eat or sleep enough," complained Mrs. Gordon, helping herself to more olives. "Always having to worry over one's figure."

Squabs on toast, asparagus, endive salad, disappeared while Mrs. Stone and Mrs. White discussed the latest scientific methods of eating to grow thin.

"Look at the girls of the Home—straight, lithe, graceful, without Swedish exercises," laughed Mrs. Hellman. "They don't play golf. They may indulge in all the desserts they can get."

"If they only knew how we have to deny ourselves—the treatments we have to go through trying to reduce—they'd be thankful!" And Mrs. Stone, half-guiltily glancing around, took another handful of nuts.

I served at the last fresh strawberries mashed and frozen in thick cream. Strawberries in January!

"I wish I had your cook," sighed Mrs. White, finishing the last spoonful.

"I've had her for years." Mrs. Hellman leaned back content-

68

edly. "I've been fortunate with all my servants. And I have Adele in any emergency. Gives her a chance to earn a little money while in Training School—and I don't have to pay her as much as the girls from the agency." *that's why working for her*

The tray I held in my hand dropped to the pantry floor.

What? Was it possible? Paying me less than the girls from the agency? Were those her principles of economy? Her idea of helping me? Mrs. Hellman, the Friend of the Working Girl—!

going back & forth c/w Mrs. Hellman
berating & leaving

Chapter Nine

If I could only have it out with her, face to face. But there was no face-to-face language between me and Mrs. Hellman. I was choked by a thousand things that I could never tell her.

I went to an agency to find out the regular pay for waitresses.

The woman at the office told me the girls were getting fifty cents an hour.

Ten cents! So she was saving on me—my benefactress—saving ten cents on me every hour! With one hand trying to help me—with the other taking advantage of my helplessness—profiting by my need. Even boasting to her friends of her triumphant economy.

On top of this I learned that the last Training School girl who assisted Miss Perkins in the Saturday morning class for the daughters of the Board of Directors had been getting a dollar an hour. Mrs. Hellman had done me a favour to give me the other girl's job. Again at forty cents an hour. This time saving on me for the good of the Home—the glory of the institution.

How could I ever explain my side to *her?* If I'd only open my mouth to talk, I'd be an ingrate. In accusing her, I'd condemn myself.

I vowed one thing—never again to be a waitress in her house. I'd starve first.

Then Arthur Hellman telephoned. What a voice! I forgot everything. Bewitched with his voice. He was giving a party in the Washington Mews Studio that he had furnished for a musician, a composer.

Arthur Hellman—music—a party of young people belonging to his world—I had to go.

What did his mother matter? What did anything else matter? Even though I was to be only a waitress. He wanted me. Needed me.

I stood with my hands over my eyes, in a daze of sunshine. I left the earth. I could not keep myself from soaring away. It was so good to let go of reason. Dream. Dream. Lose myself dreaming.

Mrs. Hellman had spoken of Jean Rachmansky. Arthur Hellman had turned a penniless, unknown musician into a star. Rachmansky had been only a steerage passenger on the same ship with Arthur Hellman. One night he had stolen up to the first-class deck in search of a piano.

Arthur Hellman, strolling in the corridor, heard music floating out of the deserted ballroom. He stopped to listen. Who was this? Instantly he felt genius. A new find.

From that moment, Jean Rachmansky ceased to be a steerage passenger. Arthur Hellman ordered a first-class cabin for him. His valet rigged him out with a new outfit. A private concert which Arthur Hellman arranged made Rachmansky the talk of the boat.

The fairy tale still whirled in my head as I got off the Washington Square bus. I searched for the address of the house. Washington Mews. What a romantic street!

Little houses in a cool, shady lane, tucked in behind big houses. Each little jewel of a house cut a bit different from the others.

71

Here, in the heart of the city, only half a block away from taxicabs and busses, was the stillness, the beauty of the country. A separate world, serene in its own atmosphere of rich silence.

Mrs. Hellman's butler answered my ring.

I caught a quick glimpse of the beautifully furnished studio. A grand piano stretched its lovely body across the end of the room. Soft rugs, low couches, colourful hangings, pictures, flowers. And in such luxury Arthur Hellman had started a penniless musician.

Arthur Hellman knew how to give with a full hand. Imagine Arthur Hellman asking Rachmansky to go bargain-hunting for sale shoes when he himself had his made to order. He wasn't a stingy philanthropist like his mother.

"Hurry up! You're needed back here."

The butler dragged me down from my high thoughts and showed me my place in the pantry. But through the opening in the screen I watched the front entrance to the living room.

A sound of voices. In came Arthur Hellman and Jean Rachmansky. Two fine, thoughtful faces, but how different! Arthur Hellman—up and alive—aware of everything around him. The other, shy, withdrawn, his gaze lost inside himself. And yet there was a follow-the-gleam look in Rachmansky's dark eyes that almost overshadowed, for a moment, Arthur Hellman's commanding presence.

Rachmansky let Arthur Hellman show him around. But when he got to the piano, he ceased trying to be interested. Absently striking a few chaotic chords, he quieted down until his fingers barely touched the keys.

"You see that painting? It's a Gauguin," Arthur Hellman explained.

"Beautiful," came from Rachmansky in a distant voice.

"What do you think of this decoration?" Hellman pointed to a gorgeous Spanish shawl thrown over the piano.

Rachmansky did not even look up. His fingers groped aimlessly, alighting on a chord here and there. Gradually, he drifted into a maze of colourful harmonies. "That's Chasin's *Procession,*" Hellman said, stepping quickly toward the piano.

I couldn't follow the melody, but the mood took possession of me.

I felt myself waking from the little hurts of my life that made Mrs. Hellman ride my shoulders like the Old Man of the Sea. Her committee luncheons, her cheap economies fled like dark shapes of a child's dream in the morning.

I was alive with a new sense of life.

Memories of Father. The way he took me to operas and concerts. Waiting on a long line for hours, in the rain and snow, only to get standing room.

Gone was the rankling irritation at having to be helped. Gone the wall between people who have and those who have not. After all, what was the difference between the grand company in there, at the piano, and me at the sink in a waitress's apron? The difference was only outside. If people could always hear such music!

Life was not what you put in your stomach, or wore on your back, or the house you lived in. It was what you felt in your heart and thought in your mind.

The vision paled. Flickered out entirely.

I realized that Rachmansky had stopped playing. I was Adele, the servant again. And the rich were the rich and the poor were the poor. And I was in the pantry, hired to wait on those lucky ones.

The guests were arriving.

Soon the room was filled with the noise of young people.

Laughter and gay voices. Beautiful dresses on slim young bodies. Weaving of gay colours against the dark, graceful figures of young men.

The pride and pleasure of a discoverer glowed in Arthur's face as he brought up person after person to his lion. Rachmansky abstractedly shook hands with them. Only a hand was there. He was far away.

"Oh, I adore Chopin!"

"Mr. Rachmansky! You Slavs have such wonderful musical souls!"

"Don't you think Tschaikowsky is your greatest composer?"

Rachmansky smiled dutifully at their attempts to talk music. At last Arthur Hellman came to the rescue. He broke through the chatter of polite emptiness. "Rachmansky isn't here to lecture on music but to play it," he said, and led him over to the piano.

They settled themselves in their chairs, ready to listen with every show of attention. Rachmansky, leaning over the keys, impatiently waited for the murmurs to subside and the last giggles to cease. Only when there was absolute silence did he begin to play.

I went on spreading the caviar over the rounds of bread. I listened to the music. It was a beautiful melody woven of sounds finer than silk, but it was not of my life. It felt thin and far away.

On the other side of the door, they seemed to enjoy it. Applause followed applause. He finished playing Chopin's Revolutionary *Etude*. Then, after a pause, Arthur Hellman announced that Rachmansky would play an original composition. It filled the room with the spirits of lost ones, seeking and groping and unable to find any goal. The whole drowning sea of poverty. The jobless. The hungry. The weak in their want knocking at the doors of the

74

charities. The girls defenseless in that Working Girls' Home, under the kind rich ladies—Rachmansky's music voiced it all.

The eyes of the audience began to wander away absently, though their bodies leaned forward in appropriate poses of attention. It had no meaning for them, this music of hunger and insecurity.

But, for me, the walls of the pantry faded again. The lettuce leaves slipped from my fingers. Pushing back my bowl, I walked out of the pantry and leaned against the door, my whole being alive with his music.

Rachmansky's face looked almost strained as he was playing. And when he stopped, he was hardly aware of the people around him. His expression changed to one of dismay as he saw everybody smiling and briskly applauding.

He bowed to the polite audience. Then he caught sight of me, solemn, unsmiling, my eyes fixed on him with the hunger of all I felt.

"Who are you?" Rachmansky's glance lingered questioningly.

I became aware of his look. I started to speak to him. There was a pull at my sleeve.

"Look here, where do you think you are?" whispered the butler. "Come on! Get on the job."

I began to arrange the trays, thinking what I would say to Rachmansky when I served him. But when I came out with the refreshments, he no longer saw me. He was surrounded by flattering ladies. They took from me cocktails, sandwiches, and saw me no more than if I were part of my tray, except one artist who, having had too many cocktails, caught my arm at the pantry door. Wabbling on unsteady feet, he breathed thickly: "Woman! Where have you been all my life? Your hair! You've got to pose for me to-morrow."

The butler came to my rescue, sending me out to gather the empty glasses.

Later on, the mood to speak to Rachmansky went from me completely. I was taken up again in the excitement of everything around me.

"I'd like another cocktail." A smooth hand reached up to my tray.

She was a clever-looking young girl, all paint and style and mocking laughter. With one eye she tried to vamp Arthur Hellman. With the other, she watched to see if she made her effect.

"Arthur, old dear! You're so wrapped up in your great works, you're forgetting all your little friends. I feel horribly neglected."

"You neglected?" He turned his head slowly toward her in mock surprise. "You? If I swallowed that, you'd tell me another."

She pulled him down beside her, his hand in both hers. "Don't you love me any more?"

"More and more, my dear."

"I honestly think that if I could convince you of my want, if I could show you my soul, ragged and starving for lack of you, you would be mine, as the books have it." She playfully tucked her arm through his.

"And what then? Would you have me, misguided as you think I am?"

"You're more than misguided, dearie. You're mad. It's in the Hellman blood—doing good to the poor. You're really as much addicted to philanthropy as your own mother, only with modern improvements."

"Poor Mother!" He made a sound that was half a laugh and

76

half a sigh. "She's honestly trying to find the wisest way to share what she has. She feels the guilt of wealth as I do."

"The awful seriousness of you—Galahad Hellman! How is your pet thief that you're reforming into your bank cashier?" [is only got R. / for own benefit]

Arthur's face lighted up. "Laugh all you want. The only thing that boy needed was a chance. And he has it."

"You with your reformed thieves and dazzling protégés—not to mention your funny mousy eyes! It's lucky you have those eyes, Arthur. Even a grand passion for the poor can't spoil them."

"Oh—Ma-r-i-o-n!"

"Yes. All your fervour for high theories and low life just makes your eyes more glimmery. Maybe you go in for the Sir Galahad stuff just because it's so becoming. Do you know, I almost wish that were the reason."

"Do you mean that?"

"Of course I do. Because, damn it all, I like you—we all do—and it makes you so alien. Like a Russian accent in what you would call your soul."

"You make me feel quite exotic."

"You are. It's part of your fatal charm. But your feet are American any way. Oh, I'm dying to dance. Have your prodigy play, *You Made Me Love You.*"

"Have a heart! Marion. Rachmansky is no jazz player."

"Poor man!"

She lit a cigarette and, through circles of smoke, gazed at Arthur with her wise, innocent smile.

The perfect art with which this young thing played at love, using so knowingly every feature of her face, every line of her figure, stabbed me with an admiration that swept out envy.

How wonderful! Like an actress on the stage, playing a part.

And, without knowing, I tilted my head into the same graceful pose.

My tray slanted suddenly. Crash went half the glasses.

"Oh—h!" Horror was on my face.

"Never mind, Adele! Accidents will happen." Arthur Hellman put a steadying hand on my arm and stooped down to help me pick up the broken bits of glass.

What did it matter how the butler bawled me out? And the ladies politely tried not to look at me. The kindness of Arthur Hellman's eyes blinded me to everything.

With head high, I started out again. This time, I kept my eyes steadily on my tray, but all I saw was Arthur Hellman. Arthur Hellman stooping down to help me. Arthur Hellman's steadying hand on my arm.

To his mother, to his sister, I was only someone hired by the hour. But Arthur Hellman made me feel a person—not a servant.

And my imagination took on one of its seven-league strides. . . . He isn't being kind to me just to be kind. It is I. . . . I interest him. . . .

What fun, what joy it was to be here! What things I was seeing and hearing while serving them with such a dumb, silent face!

"I'm bored of going from party to party. I want to do something worth while. Take up social work . . ."

It was Edna, Arthur's sister, sitting on the window ledge, her hands clasped around her knees, frowning earnestly as she talked into the bantering eyes of the young man beside her.

Her brother, coming by at the moment, stopped to join their talk.

Very slowly, I began sweeping up the cigarette ashes from a near-by table.

"Come, come, Edna," the man said. "You—you doing social work?"

"Certainly, I just finished a course in the *School of Philanthropy*. You have no idea how much is needed to be done for the poor." There was the Hellman glow of the Crusaders in her plain face. "But it's work that must be done by trained minds with scientific vision."

"Trained minds—scientific vision—" Arthur mocked. "Fine phrases—great words."

Catching sight of me, lost in listening to the conversation, he broke into a laugh. "I pity the poor victims of trained minds and scientific vision."

He was saying the words to them, but I felt he was talking to me with his eyes.

For the rest of the afternoon, the idea fixed itself in my mind that I would have to *make* a chance to talk to Arthur Hellman when he was alone. I could think of nothing but what I would say to him—what he would answer.

The playing came to an end. Rachmansky rose from the piano and tried to smile back at the shower of compliments thrown at him from all sides. But the light went from his face. The musician became the man. He looked haggard—irritable—a dark cloud in the centre of these gay young people. Very soon he left.

Gradually the crowd thinned. Then only Arthur Hellman remained. Even in the pantry, my eyes burned through the wall. I felt him there—alone. Presently I heard him at the piano.

I stepped softly to the door. How good it was to see him without other people! Everything in me rushed to him.

What wonders that man could do for me! By one little bit of

love, he could make me the equal of his sister, his mother. If I struggled for a thousand years, could I ever get into his world? Only the magic of his love could get me there.

I put down my tray and leaned over the piano.

He looked up and smiled. His eyes had that curious shine, both cold and warm, that burned through my dumbness, my fear. I heard myself speaking.

"I love to hear you play."

"Why, Adele, I'm only an amateur."

"Oh, but your touch is like fingers on the heart."

His hands lifted from the keys a moment. I thought he was going to stop, but he went on with his playing.

"I didn't know you were so fond of music."

"Oh, music! And you—you playing it."

"Well—that's rather a wild statement."

"Is it wild to say what I feel?"

Arthur Hellman stopped his playing with a jerk. A look of annoyance chilled his eyes. But the next moment his face broke into a smile: "Adele, I'm afraid you flatter me too much. Don't you think you had better finish clearing the room and run along? Thanks awfully."

I felt hit with a club in the back of my head.

I picked up the tray and stumbled out.

It came back to me, that day months ago when, with a heart full of gratitude, I rushed with open arms to kiss his mother. The look of revulsion on Mrs. Hellman's face had come back to stare at me from her son's. Only for a moment. But in that moment all my dreams crashed.

They were all alike. Arthur Hellman was his mother's son. . . .

Chapter Ten

T he Home was all dressed up, spick and span for the show. Every door of every room was open. You could see at a glance smooth, white beds, spotless bureau covers, chairs and tables set exactly in the right place for the picture. The whole house and we girls in it were turned into a public exhibition, in honour of the annual Board of Directors' meeting. Even the dinner was a special company dinner, planned to make us look happy for the show-off.

The whole troop of Board of Director ladies were going through the house—shining ladies bountiful—rejoicing in all they had done for us.

At least once a year we, who had no more to say in the running of the Home than the dumb tables and chairs, were important enough to be looked over, smiled at, patted by all the donors and patrons and contributors.

In the domestic science department were display tables of breads, cakes, puddings, and salads which we had prepared. A housekeeping room where bed-making, furnishing, and cleaning a home were shown in a row of little dolls' houses.

In the social hall were charts in different coloured inks. A muddle of figures and lines about the number of meals and the number of beds and the number of girls in the house. But Mrs.

Hellman was pointing out to her friends a red line in the biggest chart: "See that peak of progress? What strides the Home has made the last five years."

Then, she greeted me with her ever-ready smile: "Good-evening, my dear. So you're going to speak for us to-night. That will be very interesting."

"You are very kind, Mrs. Hellman."

My voice was low and dutiful, but within, I felt, "Yes. Yes. Add my speech to the rest of the bunk."

I ran up to my room, slammed the door, opened wide the window. A cool wind blew over my forehead. A little calmer, I sat down at my table.

There was the morning's newspaper with the article about the Home. I glanced at the picture of Mrs. Hellman and myself. Underneath it, "The Founder of the Home with One of the Girls She Has Befriended."

Yesterday, when the reporter came, I hadn't the nerve to refuse posing with Mrs. Hellman. How I despised myself for my cowardice!

Would I never have the courage to tell them what I felt? When Miss Simons asked me to prepare a speech of gratitude, why didn't I have the guts to speak up and get out of it somehow? What would happen to me if I dared let loose my black heart?

By the time I got downstairs again, the Board of Directors and their invited guests had assembled on the platform of the social hall. That was the signal for us to take our seats and stop talking. In eager silence, we craned our necks to catch a glimpse of those important people who were going to tell the public about the Working Girls' Home and what it meant in the world.

The judge was there. And the mayor. His Honour had come a

little early, and began shaking hands. He shook hands with Mrs. Hellman and the rest of the Board of Directors. Then he began shaking hands with the girls and kept it up till the meeting started with the arrival of the chairman.

A little out of breath from being late, but flushed with the importance of the occasion, the chairman introduced the mayor. "We have the greatest good fortune to have with us to-day the man who has done more than any other mayor to make our city great. He is a man who understands the common people. He is of the people and for the people. We have with us here the Abraham Lincoln of our day!"

Bowing and flourishing his hand in a respectful salute, he pointed to the beaming mayor.

His Honour cleared his throat, breathed "ahem" twice in deep, rich tones as he rose to his feet.

"My heart is with the Working Girl," he boomed. "I always have done and always will do everything in my power for the people, the common, hard-working, honest people, the backbone of America."

Then he went on with increasing passion: "Those of you who read the papers dominated by the Interests know how savagely I've been attacked for serving the public. But they cannot frighten me. They'll never drive me out of office. I'll continue to do good. I'll continue to be the servant of you all." And he pointed a thick finger from girl to girl.

How could we help smiling up at him? A fine man with a fancy tailored suit—our servant! The first servant we'd ever had. The applause rang on long after he had taken his seat.

The mayor looked anxiously at his watch. He turned to Mrs. Hellman with a worried smile. "I must ask to be excused," he whispered, "I have an address to make before the United Bridge Engineers of Brooklyn." Then he tiptoed out, leaving us to enjoy the other speakers.

The judge was a kind old man. He almost made us forget the Home with his funny stories. But not for long. Up got the chairman and began a long-winded introduction of our patron saint.

"Mrs. Hellman's name will go down to the ages for her service to humanity." On and on he went, finally ending with: "We shall now have the pleasure of hearing the Ideals of the Home expounded by the noble woman who has founded it."

All perfect, in her quiet, expensive clothes, Mrs. Hellman bowed to the chairman and to the audience. Then in her soft, low voice:

"I feel there is no service for the poor more urgently needed than the Working Girls' Home of the kind we have established. Here, the eager young girls who come to us have a chance to escape from their cramped surroundings to wider, more desirable conditions, where they can expand and express themselves. One of our own girls has called this Home an 'oasis in the wilderness.'"

Then came something I hadn't counted on—something I wasn't prepared to face. Like an avenging ghost—my old letter of gratitude that I had thought safely buried by the months. That terrible lie—a lie all the more terrible because it had once been truth. Mrs. Hellman picked up the letter, held it between careful fingers. "We cherish this," she said, "as one of our most precious documents."

When she finished reading it, the cheering and handclapping were even louder than for the mayor.

Then I heard my name. The chairman was saying: "And now, ladies and gentlemen, I am going to call on a girl who is a true

84

untrue!

product of this institution. She came to us homeless, friendless, without work. And here she found not only home, friends, and work, but the inspiration to raise herself to become a teacher of her own people. Her appreciation and gratitude for the benefits she has received have won for her the chance to go to Training School. I want this young lady to tell you what living here has meant to her. I take great pleasure in introducing to you Miss Adele Lindner."

I had learned the speech by heart. My nervousness, my stage fright vanished as I heard my voice fall upon the room. I almost forgot, in the pleasure of hearing myself, the lies I was saying. "How can I begin to put into words the thanks I owe to the ladies for all they have done for me in this institution? I have so much to be grateful for. My food, my clothes, my chance to become a teacher, a worker in the world—everything I owe to Mrs. Hellman and the generous friends who have been so kind to me, so wisely planned out my future. I speak not only for myself, but for all the girls who—"

Then I saw Arthur Hellman come in. He took his seat beside the chairman.

There was a stir among the girls. A flutter among the ladies.

My voice faltered and came to a stop.

What did it mean, this crowd of people? Why was I here? What had I been saying?

I looked at Arthur Hellman. Cool. Calm. Perfect.

The musicale. His cold eyes. "Don't you think you had better finish clearing the room and run along?" sounded again in my ears.

Why is he better than I? Why is he free to say what he feels? Why must I say these lies?

he's rich

85

The written speech crumpled in my hand. "It's a lie. I'm not grateful. I hate this Home. I hate myself for living here. I hate the hand-me-down rags I wear on my back. I hate every damned bit of kindness you've ever done me. I'm poisoned—poisoned with the hurts, the insults I suffered in this beastly place."

I stopped, panting. I felt my eyes were ablaze. My hands clenched. Red spots burned on my cheeks.

There was a horrified hush. Then all was confusion.

Faces stared at me, shocked and breathless. Sounds of nervous laughter. Voices from all sides crying at me. "Crazy!" "Oh-h-h-h!" "Shame!"

One voice, sharp and excited, screamed out: "The truth! Give it to them, Adele! Hit them another crack!"

"Thank God I'm not a lady, so I can tell you to your faces in my own language what I think of you! Hypocrites! Shaming me before strangers—boasting of your kindness—because I had no home—I had no friends—I had no work. Feeding your vanity on my helplessness—my misfortune. Right before the whole world—you had to pull the dirt out of the ash can. You had to advertise to all—'Remember, beggar, where you would have been if it hadn't been for us!'

"Shylocks! A pound of flesh you want for every ounce of help—worse than Shylocks! Shylock only wanted the man's flesh. You want his soul. You robbed me of my soul, my spirit. You robbed me of myself. When I hated you, I had to smile up to you, and flatter you—"

Somebody seized me by the arm and tried to pull me down. I wrenched free, leaping up like a wild person. "Gratitude you want? For what? Because you forced me to become your flunkey—your servant? Because you crushed the courage out of me when I

86

was out of a job? Forced me to give up my ambition to be a person and learn to be your waitress—?

"Humbugs! Go play bridge to save your orphans! Stick to your facial treatments—and massage—and eating to grow thin. But don't dabble in the suffering of lives you know nothing about!

"Hellman Home! Burn it! Tear it down! Better for the girls to walk the streets than to suffer your monkey business any longer!"

"She's gone crazy!"

"Why didn't you leave if you didn't like it?"

That cry from one of the girls brought me to a stop. I sank back without breath.

Everything swam before me in a jumble. Through the riot and uproar I saw with acute clearness the fixed row of astounded eyes on the platform.

I saw Arthur Hellman make a motion toward me. I did not wait to find out what he'd do. Somehow, I got out of there. Up to my room.

And then, shaking my fist in the air, I thought of all the things I could have said and lost the chance of saying.

"Publicity Hounds! Why this holler about the Working Girl when all you're after is your pictures in the paper?

"What right have a bunch of fat rich women to set themselves up as Big Sisters of the Working Girl? Sisters!

"Millions to charity with one hand—with the other—cheating *hypocrisy* me ten cents.

"Daring to tell us how we should dress—what we should eat— how we should save! Dictating to us—Preaching to us—maddening us with their penny saved—penny earned!

"You've shown me up for a beggar! So I've shown you up for the humbugs you are!"

- making them be shameful for
being poor ... constantly reminding
them of what they are

My voice suddenly stopped in my throat. There, in the door, stood Mrs. Hellman and Miss Simons, their faces white and frightened.

"My dear"—Mrs. Hellman came toward me—she touched my forehead—"this is delirium. The girl is burning with fever."

"Adele!" Miss Simons gasped. "What has happened to you? Have you gone mad?"

"Mad? I'm sane for the first time in my life. I'll cringe and flatter no longer. I'll tell you what you are—a hired stepmother—a servant of the saviours."

Mrs. Hellman just stared at me, her eyes dark with wounded sorrow. Her mouth opened as if to speak. But she didn't say anything. She looked slumped and tired, like an old woman, after a hard day's work.

I walked right by her and by Miss Simons, my head high in the air. That I had hurt them only added to my savage exaltation.

The girls stopped me in the hall, pulling at me, shouting excitedly. I could hardly struggle free from their clutching hands.

When I got outside, Mrs. Hellman had just stepped into her car. Her son was about to go in after her. He saw me. Then he leaned forward and said something to his mother.

The car moved on without him and he started toward me.

I wouldn't wait for him. I hurried away. I felt him following me. He caught me by the arm and pulled me to a stop. "Adele! Wait! Where are you going? You can't run away like this."

I just walked on, and he kept step after me.

"Adele! I didn't know you had the grit!"

All the strength suddenly went from me. My knees ached. I felt as tired as Mrs. Hellman looked.

Arthur Hellman caught my hand in his, gently stroked my

fingers. "You know I'm your friend. I understand why you did it. I want you to feel I'm with you. You've got more spunk than I thought any girl could have."

I hated him. I hated his mother. I hated all the Hellmans. I jerked free and started to run.

"This running away is childish. Listen to me. You need someone to look after you. I know I could help you." *trying to help again so she didn't want*

I couldn't make any answer come. My throat felt pierced with knives.

"Adele! It was a knockout! You kicked the bottom out of their shams! You showed them up. The way you put it over—magnificent drama! Can't you feel, dear, I'm *really with you*? Girl, you're great!"

At last words came. They sounded hoarse and queer. "Get away, can't you? I can't bear the sight of you. I hate you!"

"I can't let you go like this. My dear, this is not the way to treat me. Let's get a taxi. We'll ride around in the park—anywhere."

Still concerned about himself His eyes were soft and tender. But I didn't care. He, too, had hurt me—insulted me. To him, too, I was only a charity.

He turned, waved his stick at a taxi.

That was my chance. I saw a subway entrance. I rushed in.

I wanted to take a train. Just ride anywhere.

Then I realized I had no purse. Not even a nickel for carfare.

I got back to the crowded street. Suddenly I found I was sobbing aloud. I could not stop my tears.

I wandered on—on. Where? I did not know.

Then I found myself in a station house. A matron was asking me questions.

I crumpled over on the bench. A lost, dumb thing, crying and crying and crying.

No reform affection 89

All that night, on the cot in the station house, torrents of tears kept pouring down my cheeks, washing away the bitterness, the hate, the lost dream of the Home, of Arthur Hellman.

In the morning, my eyes were dry. There were no more tears. I could never feel again. Never get excited about anything. Never again be glad. Never again be sad or sorry. My burning ambitions were dead. I was at the bottom, where the outcome of things up there, in the world, no longer mattered.

Chapter Eleven

irty tenements—row after row. Sunken in monotony. Smudged with gloom. Tired. Sagging. Like the gray-brown faces of workers returning at the end of the day.

Scrawled, careless signs: "Girls Wanted" . . . "Hands Wanted." . . . The signs loomed up—grabbing at me—dragging me back—to the dirt, the noise, the confusion from which I had tried to escape.

Operators on Hemstitching Machines:
Paid while Learning

I was so hungry—anything for something to eat.

Up three flights of stairs, I opened a huge iron door, looked into a roaring bedlam of machines. Girls—men—young—old—driving—driven—machines all!

Oh, no. I couldn't do that.

I turned away, stumbled down to the street. At the corner, I stopped in front of a Dairy Restaurant. My eyes devoured the whole pyramid of apples and cakes in the window. Then I saw a sign, "Dishwasher Wanted."

I stepped boldly in. "You want a dishwasher?"

The woman at the desk took me in with a look. "It's eight dollars a week and meals."

Eight dollars? How could I live on that? But I followed her through the swinging doors into the kitchen.

She put a heaping dish of food before me. "Go to it, young one! But don't you walk out on me and leave the dishes."

Little by little, I took in the things around me. With each mouthful, I saw more clearly the sweaty cooks, the greasy pots and pans.

Loud voices of waiters shouting orders: "*Gefülte* fish!" "*Borsht* and cheese *blintzes!*" "Chopped herring and onions!"

My ravenous gulping laid bare the coarse plate. The knife and fork, bent, rusty. The food, which a moment before smelled and tasted so appetizing, now stuck in my throat.

Dulled by the dead air of frying and steaming, I settled back in my chair. My eyes closed.

From under my shut lids, slowly, bit by bit, Mrs. Hellman's dining room came before me. It was a long way from that Fifth Avenue house of hers to this Second Avenue hash joint.

"Say, if you're waiting for coffee and cigarettes, forget it." The boss came along, motioned me to the sink where an old woman stood patiently scraping dish by dish. "Jazz it up! They're waiting for clean dishes."

I wanted to get out. The shrivelled old woman bent over the pile of greasy plates gave me the creeps. But there stood the boss. I had had my dinner.

With gritted teeth, I plunged my hand into the scummy water and began to wash.

It seemed to me that for ages upon ages I stood there at the sink, washing endless stacks of dishes. The humped bunch of rags shuffling on unsteady feet kept piling up more dishes. With my back turned, I felt her eyes following me about, talking away at me. I couldn't hear. I couldn't answer.

At last—an end to the day. The old woman slid the last dish on the shelf. Her shaking hand reached for her rusty old coat.

"Where live you?"

"No place," I answered.

Then she turned, shook me almost roughly by the arm. "What is with you the matter?" Her sharp gaze bored into me. "You don't listen to nothing. But I don't know—I can't let you go from my eyes. Come only along." She tugged at me. "Here—put yourself on your hat—button together your coat. *Nu*—make already, quick."

I couldn't bear to have her touch me. What a worn-out old face! The shrunken, toothless mouth. Wrinkles knotting into wrinkles. Old enough for the grave.

My God! This impossible old creature was hauling me away as if she had always known me. And I was too tired to resist.

Allen Street. A crowded stoop of people. Groping to a basement. A mattress. I dropped the weary weight of my body. As I drowsed off, I felt somebody covering me, tucking me in warm. Then I slept the dead sleep of exhaustion.

I woke. I knew it was six in the morning. The old habit of rising at the same hour every day, at the Home, was like an alarm clock in me.

I raised myself on my elbow. Where was I? A high tenement wall shut out sun and air. Only a gray reflection of light squeezed itself down from the airshaft above. Windows like bars. A zigzag of rusty fire escapes.

My eyes turned back to the room. Paper ripped from the wall. The low ceiling cracked and stained from leaking pipes. Ragged bits of cotton from the torn comforter clung to my hands. Nothing could be poorer than this dingy basement. Mrs. Hershbein's place was a palace to this.

The noises told me what was happening in the surrounding flats—" Aby! Aby! A black year on you! Get up already!"—"Mrs. Klinger! It's my wash line! What freshness! Her dirty featherbed over my head."—"Mamma! Mamma! Aby punched me in the jaw!" . . .

Through the half-open door, I saw the old woman peacefully bent over the washtub, near the hot kitchen stove, unmindful of all the noise outside. A warm, homey smell of suds filled the air. There was something so familiar and reassuring in the steady rub, rub, rub of the washboard. The song without words of the poor. Her leaning forward and pulling back at the tub was as soothing as rocking a child to sleep in the dusk. A long-forgotten picture of my own mother flashed up in me. My own mother in our old kitchen.

I got up and groped for my clothes. But I couldn't find all my things.

The rubbing stopped for a moment. The shrill, cracked voice called, "Your waist you want—what? Here is it. I got already it washed out—by the stove."

"You? Oh, why did you?"

I started to get it. Why did she do that? This funny, strange old woman.

She turned from the tub, one hand rubbing her back. "Better go wash yourself. And here yet is my Sabbath towel. *Nu!* Make quick—only!"

The ironed-out towel with the fresh, clean smell was old as the old woman herself. The only whole thing in that house. "It's too good to be used," I said.

94

"Too good! Look only—what's telling me too good! I'm in this house yet the missus." Then, softening her tone, her shaking hand stroked my hair. "Not every day falls on me the pleasure—a young girl for my guest."

I looked at her face as it broke into a million wrinkles of a smile. Everything about her as gray as the suds in the washtub. Gray skin, gray stringy hair, gray rags. It had seemed to me nothing on earth could be as terrible as to grow so old and so bent. And yet she could smile like that. Smile and receive me with that warm, rich friendliness of a person who feels she has much to give.

compare w/ rich people's attitude

"You're making me feel so at home, Mrs.—Mrs.—what shall I call you?"

"They all call me Muhmenkeh."

I took the waist that Muhmenkeh's old hands had washed and ironed, as if it was something done for me every day. I didn't want to spoil it with the worn words "thank you."

"I got a granddaughter in your years," she confided. "When I see blue eyes and red hair in a young face—it gives a pull in me—my grandchild. That's why it cut me by the heart to see you so worried and alone."

She reached to the bureau for a picture in a fancy brass frame. "Give only a look! Here she is—Shenah Gittel, my granddaughter."

It was a plain girl in a clumsy, homemade dress. But Muhmenkeh looked so proud of her I felt myself seeing through her eyes. "She's beautiful," I said.

"Ai-ai-ai! Is she yet beautiful! Long years on her! So far away in Poland. Every New Year holiday I send her away a present." Her voice lowered as if she ushered me into the secret dream of her life. "Now I'm yet saving myself for her a ticket to America. God should only let me live long enough to see her here, in good luck."

She took from the shelf a battered tomato can and shook it in my face. "Hear only! How it rings my hope—my savings' bank!"

At the jingle of the coins, two lights flamed up in Muhmenkeh's eyes. The lights spread over her face till I, too, was swept into the child gladness of her heart.

From that moment, the old woman dropped away. I saw only her eyes. That gentle, unworldly gaze. Something kept drawing me to her—making me feel underneath the things she said and did.

How she adored Shenah Gittel. She talked on and on about her. Suddenly she broke off. "God should only watch over her there in the old country. But the while we got to eat here."

She wiped her sudsy hands with her apron, and we sat down to breakfast. A pot of coffee. A tin of condensed milk. A loaf of bread. A pan of oatmeal. Cups without handles. The tablecloth a newspaper.

Muhmenkeh talked as she sawed off slices of bread. "Seventy-six years old I'll be next *Shabes*. Long years on us all. My hands lift themselves to the sky that I did not yet fall into the Old People's Home."

Her voice dropped into a whisper. "Not often comes on me such luck—a whole day's work. They want young hands and feet for a regular job." She pointed to a basket with packages of tea and coffee. "My little pushcart," her arms encircled her wares. "But I don't stand dumb in the street, waiting for them to come and buy. I knock from house to house. One day I earn something. Another day not." She looked about the little room with shining thankfulness. "God is yet good. With what bitter sweat I struggle for each cent I earn, but it's all my own—this place—when I pay my rent."

Smiling, she fell into thinking, the silence growing between us like a bond of blood. There flowed over me a sense of peace, of homecoming. Here was the real world I knew. The familiar things that made me feel secure, the washtub, the boiler of clothes on the cook stove, the newspaper for tablecloth. And over it all—Muhmenkeh.

I just stared at her. Seventy-six years old and standing on her own feet. And I beggared my soul stretching out my hands for help! Help from a Mrs. Hellman and an Arthur Hellman. Before I knew it, I found myself pouring out to her the whole mix-up of my life. "How I wasted my young years trying to catch on to the false shine of the rich—only to come back to the beginnings of myself."

"Wasted? *Nu-nu!* Wasted? What a talk! And you—a smart girl!"

Muhmenkeh rocked herself back and forth gently. She fell again into a silence. Some amusing memory quirked up all the little wrinkles of her face. When she spoke again, she drew my hand into the astonishing warmth of her two little gnarled old hands. "Listen only—child what you are—with your cry on wasted life. Take only into your young head this old, old *Bube Meise* that my grandmother used to tell me—how it's all for the best.

"One of our great rabbis—Rabbi Akiba they called him. Once Rabbi Akiba travelled himself far away from home. All what he had in the world, he carried along with him. A light with which to study the Holy Torah, a rooster to cry him awake in the early morning.

"One night, he wandered through a strange village where nobody knew him. Everybody shut on him the door right in his face. 'It's all for the best,'" said Rabbi Akiba.

"In a black and lonely forest, he fell himself asleep. Suddenly, rose up a wind and blew out his light. Came along a fox. Down he

97

swallowed the rooster in one bite. When Rabbi Akiba woke up, saw only a tail feather from his rooster left, he lifted his hands to the sky—'It's all for the best.'

"While he was yet praying himself to God, a terrible wailing tore up the air. A gang of robbers fell on the village and killed out all the people. Then Rabbi Akiba knew God was holding him in His Own Hand when nobody wanted to take him in."

Muhmenkeh held up her finger at me. A twinkle danced in the corner of her eye. "See you already—how it's yet for the best that a smart girl like you should have to hear out a foolish old story from a foolish old woman like me?"

"Oh, Muhmenkeh—Muhmenkeh! Compliments you want yet?" I cried, throwing my arms around her.

A quaint, queer pair we looked. We didn't even hear the door open until a voice wailed: "Oi-i-i! Woe is me! Muhmenkeh! To all my troubles yet, I got to stop from everything to take Sammy to the dispensary to pull out his tooth. Can I leave the baby by you, on the floor?"

"Why do you ask yet? Do I have a carpet should spoil? Or fancy dishes to break?"

Before the woman was out of sight, the baby had crawled straight across the floor to the pan of ashes.

Muhmenkeh handed me a slice of bread and butter for the child. "Go, give her, or she'll eat the ashes."

"Look only at her face and hands!"

"What's a little dirt on a child? It'll wash away before she's old enough to get married." She took two spoons and beat them together before the baby's eyes till it laughed and jumped up grabbing for them. "*Nu!* What fails the little heart? Long years on her! All she needs is a little bit of luck."

What was that little bit of luck, I wondered? Where could you find it? Peace—rest—it was still so far from me.

Muhmenkeh turned back to her wash. She opened the window and hung the clothes on the line.

"Did you eat, already, Muhmenkeh?" A woman called from across the air shaft.

"Eat yet? Let me alone from eating. Am I the landlord's wife, I should eat myself an hour for breakfast? But you—you want maybe a cup of coffee? Come in. Come in."

The woman, with hips like pillows, waddled in. In her hand was a plate covered with a dish towel. "Give only a guess. What's hiding here for you?"

"*Gefülte* fish?"   _different kind of sharing / help

"*Gefülte* fish on plain Monday? You think I'm a millionaire? Her hand stroked the towel, ready for a feat of magic. With a grand flourish, the towel came off. A thick slice of hot fried herring and onion, sizzling in its own fat! "For you. Hold it maybe for your dinner. What?"

"Wait so long?" Muhmenkeh clapped her hands, seeing how my eyes popped out of my head for a bite of this treat. "We'll have a *sooda* right away."

On my way to work, the whole street looked new. The freshness of the morning breathed a new wonder over the old street. The dirty, squeezed-in tenements lost their worries and cares. Like people with a new chance, they lifted their heads and spread themselves out in the sun. A sudden clearness came to me. I felt close to all things living.

Funny, strange old Muhmenkeh. What was that something behind her eyes tugging at me—drawing me on?

99

Chapter Twelve

For a while I made myself insensitive to the terrible air of the kitchen. I hardened myself not to smell the smelly sink. I stood there washing the dishes, my mind miles away from what my hands were doing.

A headache began pounding in me. My bones ached. But I kept on my feet for days. Suddenly, as I turned on a fresh stream of steaming water, I dropped to the floor, the dishes crashing from my hands.

Somehow, I got back to Muhmenkeh. "I'm all in," I said, slumping into the first chair.

"Oi weh! The flu is going around the city. You maybe are yet catching it already."

Anxious, bewildered, she stood over me. "The while maybe a hot glass of tea with a lot of sugar and lemon." She hurried over to the stove—with amazing swiftness, mixed a hot drink for me. I could barely swallow a spoonful at a time. My throat hurt, my chest, too, I couldn't draw a breath.

"Maybe it's not good enough warm, my covers? Wait only— I'll give a look around by the neighbours what something warm I can find."

Before I had finished my tea, Muhmenkeh had returned with a huge red featherbed which she tucked around me.

The next day my head felt like a ton. The outside of me burning and inside I was shivering with cold.

My God! If I really got sick—how could I throw myself on this poor old woman? A dull, aching stupor drowned my question. Weakness crippled my hands and feet. I ceased to struggle. Ceased to care what happened to me.

Moments of consciousness. Gradually these moments lengthened. Muhmenkeh always waiting on me. Cooling my forehead. Straightening my pillow. Something constantly feeding me.

One morning I woke up. My senses clear. Clearer than health. I saw Muhmenkeh bent over me, unearthly gentleness looking out of her brown, wrinkled face. "Child! You'll live! You're better already. He said it'll come that way, the doctor. You'll wake yourself up and right away you'll know me."

That something behind her eyes. In that moment of newborn clarity I looked right into it. She stood there caught up in one ray of sunlight like something sainted. Unearthly. Her whole body as luminous as her eyes.

Weakness still held me silent. I had so much to say to Muhmenkeh, but not in words, only with my eyes.

I lay back watching Muhmenkeh bring me breakfast. Medicine. Bathing my face and hands. How long have I been like this? When did she work? From where did the money come?

The first time I sat up Muhmenkeh said: "Maybe to-day a little chicken soup I'll cook you? Yes—*mein kind?*"

She took from the shelf the battered tomato can. Her bank. Shook out a few coins on the table. Then, throwing a shawl over her head, slipped out.

So Muhmenkeh had been taking the money out of her bank all the time I was ill. The money she had earned with such sweat, saved a penny to a penny for her grandchild. And she had spent it on me—a stranger.

I had to know how much she had spent on me. I staggered over to the chair. After a pause, I gathered enough strength to stand up, reached the shelf for the bank. I looked in. Only a few nickels and dimes left.

Muhmenkeh returned. I lay back silent, watching her put the pot on the stove. "While it's cooking your soup, I'll give a run out with my little pushcart, and Mrs. Mirsky will hold you company till I come back."

Mrs. Mirsky came in. The baby in one arm. A loaf of bread in the other. In both her hands she clutched her apron with half-peeled potatoes.

"*Gott sei dank* you're better! Long years on us all," she greeted, setting the baby on the floor.

She had no sooner begun peeling the potatoes when Benny and Sammy tumbled in, ragged, barefoot, their faces smeared with the mud of the gutters.

"Mamma! I'm hungry!"

"Hungry!" echoed the other.

"Wolves! Wild Indians! When will I have a little rest from your eating?" shrilled the mother, shoving a thick slice of bread into each of their hands.

Minnie, with her red pigtail tied with a shoe string, skipped in and joined the hungry chorus. "I'm dying for a bite. What's to eat—Mamma?"

They were gulping the bread greedily when, suddenly, like dogs drawn to the smell of a bone, they leaped over to the stove. "Chicken! Gee whiz! Chicken! By golly! Chicken!"

"Devils! Gluttons! Who wants you here? Ain't the street big enough for you?"

Mrs. Mirsky tried to shoo them out, but in vain. With gaping, watering mouths and glistening eyes they hung about the boiling pot.

I struggled over to the sink, washed and dressed. The effort so exhausted me that I had to slump back on the bed to rest.

The boys began playing cowboys racing on horseback. Then they turned into Indian chiefs dancing about the tribal pot. Minnie skipped her rope in time to their dance. Her eyes bright, her nostrils quivering with the odour of the steaming chicken. Even the baby bobbed up and down, excited by the warm, rich smell.

In spite of all this clamour, I slept.

When I awoke, Mrs. Mirsky brought me a cup of soup. Four pair of hungry eyes, four hungry mouths devoured the chicken soup I held in my hand.

"Here, take it, Benny." I handed it to the oldest. "You divide it evenly among you all."

Four mouths strained to sip the one cup of soup at the same time. With a crash, it went to the floor. Like yelping savages they fought to lick up the precious drops of soup from the broken pieces, while Mrs. Mirsky topped their cries: "Wolves! Devils! Gluttons! I should only live to get rid of you all in one day!— Minnie! *Oi weh!* You'll cut yourself yet with that piece!" Grabbing up the baby in her arms, she cooed over it. "*Tzireleh!* Little heart! Did you hurt yourself, darling?"

Through all this tumult I heard a low voice, "Adele!"

That voice. I knew it was Arthur Hellman. I knew it before I looked up. He stood in the open doorway, slim and straight. The same Arthur Hellman outwardly, but with an anxious, disturbed expression I had never seen before.

"Thank God, I've found you!"

I stared at him in amazement. He here? How did he find me? Why did he come? The sudden excitement of seeing him was too much for me. Faint and dizzy, I crumpled up against the pillow. Before I could pull myself together, the children surrounded him. Mrs. Mirsky gave him a suspicious glance. "Are you maybe from the Charities, yet?"

"No, I'm not from the Charities."

"Gee! He's a truant officer," said Benny. "Let's beat it." They fled like frightened rabbits.

"Are you maybe from the Board of Health?" ventured Mrs. Mirsky again.

"No. I'm an old friend of Miss Lindner."

Mrs. Mirsky picked up the baby and, with a backward glance over her shoulder, shuffled out.

language of poor is diferent

Chapter Thirteen

He shut the door and leaned his back against it. Little drops of perspiration came out on his forehead. He took out his handkerchief, dabbed his face with it, crumpled it into a tight ball.

"My God! How I've hunted for you!" He threw aside his stick and stepped toward me, holding out both his hands. "Why, you've been sick—you're still sick. Don't try to get up, Adele."

He brought a chair close to my cot.

"How I've suffered! I had to find you—Adele! I'm here to do everything possible for you." His face grew more anxious as he looked at me. "But you can't stay here. I tell you what—you must get out of here at once. I know of a splendid private sanitarium in the country. It's beautiful there. You'd love it. Yes. We must get you away."

I shrank back. "Out of here? Away from Muhmenkeh?"

"Who is Muhmenkeh?"

"Muhmenkeh? Oh, I can't tell you in words. She's sort of a godmother, grandmother of lost ones. But wait till you meet her. You can't tag her or pigeonhole her into this or that. She just *is*—"

There was a sound at the door. We both turned our heads. Bent to one side by the weight of her basket, she stumbled in. So frail and old, a wind could have blown her away.

Surprised, he looked at her. Then he rose.

"A friend from Adele?" she greeted, taking us in at a glance. "Sit yourself down, Mister."

"Yes. I'm her friend. I'm horrified to see how ill she is. This is no place for her."

He walked up and down, his hands deep in his pockets.

"Good luck on her if she only finds a place better," came from Muhmenkeh without a trace of resentment.

"Leave you, Muhmenkeh? Never."

"But, my dear, you can't get well here." He appealed to Muhmenkeh. "Don't you think she needs more comfort to get well?"

"Where best she likes it, there best she gets well."

"Let me at least call my doctor."

"I had one from the hospital."

"Let his doctor come already," said Muhmenkeh, with her eternal tolerance. "He might quicker get you up."

Arthur gave Muhmenkeh a grateful look. Grabbing his hat, he dashed off. "I'll send someone you'll surely like," he called back over his shoulder.

He sent Dr. Sirowich, the most-loved man of the East Side. A nurse was with him, but I hardly saw her at first. Just the sight of his health-giving face made me feel better.

"This is Miss Eden, who will take care of you."

"Please—but I don't want a nurse."

"Why?" He put his hand on my wrist to take my pulse. The friendly warmth of his fingers flowed through me like new health. "Why, my dear?"

"Oh, if you knew what a spick-and-span uniform does to me!"

He whispered something to Miss Eden. She nodded, smiling, and turned to go.

At the door she bumped into Arthur Hellman, his arms loaded with bundles. His face radiant with the joy of doing good. The same high purpose in the air around him as when he introduced Jean Rachmansky, the poor musician, to his friends.

"Why did the nurse go?" he asked. "Didn't you like her? Wasn't she good enough?"

"Too good for me. I'd be nervous with her around."

He smiled gently at me and turned to the doctor. "How about it, Doctor? Don't you think she ought to have a trained—"

"She's got the best nurse to be had on the East Side." And he gave Muhmenkeh's cheek a little loving pinch. "We've worked together on some pretty tough cases, haven't we, Muhmenkeh?"

Arthur began undoing his bundles. A great bunch of long-stemmed roses in my arms. Cherries, plums, oranges in a pile on the table. In one hand, he held up a bunch of hothouse grapes. In the other, a jar of chicken broth.

Dr. Sirowich smiled whimsically at him. "You look like a typical Lord Bountiful in a Christmas story." Then he pulled him over into a corner. I could hear part of his whispering. "Sanitarium—out of her element—lonely. Do the little things you can do here—with your hands, your heart. They'll help more than your money."

The unreality of the next few days will always remain in my memory. Arthur Hellman turned into a messenger boy. Running errands for Muhmenkeh. Bringing medicine. Washing dishes. Cleaning the sink. Arthur Hellman, in his English clothes, sleeves rolled up—wearing Muhmenkeh's old, patched apron. Sir Galahad armed in calico!

How earnest, how conscientious he was in awkwardness! He who could, without any fuss or feathers, supervise the arrange-

107

ments of the most elaborate entertainments was thrown into a panic when he had to attend personally to such small details as heating milk or toasting bread.

There he stood by the kitchen table, mopping the nervous sweat from his forehead with one hand, with the other trying to cut thin slices of bread.

With the most profound concentration, he arranged the two slices on the toaster, lit the flame under the saucepan of milk. Then he began to level off a teaspoonful of salt, cutting it with a knife into a half, a quarter, an eighth, then meticulously dividing the eighth into a sixteenth.

"You'll never make a cook," I laughed. "You're too conscientiously careful."

"I have to be. It's an affair of state. If I measure three grains of salt too much, I may halt our cure."

"You're so exact with the salt," I warned, "you're letting the toast burn."

"There go my good intentions." He seized the flaming slice, dropped it into the sink. Shaking the fork at me, he came over to my cot. "You're not a good executive to permit such an incompetent in your service."

"There—look!" I cried. "The milk is boiling over while you're being impertinent to your boss. You're fired."

He rushed to the stove to save the milk. "I think a cook must be the cleverest person in the world."

"It's cleverer to hire someone to cook for you."

"I think less of my education than I used to," he apologized, setting the tray before me with painstaking solemnity.

"Never mind, even King Alfred burned the cakes."

108

"And got boxed in the ears for it. That's what I deserve."

"If everyone got what he deserved," I said, "where would I be?"

"I'll tell you." He came toward me—

"Say, Mister! Is it yet time to scratch the milk pan?" The Mirsky children burst in.

Arthur looked guilty. "Oh, kids! It's a darn shame! An accident happened. But there's enough left on the side of the pan to give you each a lick."

"Oh, shucks!" they cried, attacking the pan with their spoon. But even the most vigorous of scratching couldn't wrest more than the burned bitterness of the scorch.

"Gee! That's some swell feed you gave us," they complained.

But, in spite of Arthur's bungling that cheated them out of their promised treat, they stabbed at him affectionately with their spoons. And then a general roughhousing began.

The way he sparred back, countering their enthusiastic blows with his arm, showed how fully he understood their loss and their forgiveness.

That evening, when Muhmenkeh picked up her basket to go out with her peddling, Arthur's lips tightened. He dropped the pan he was washing and stopped her at the door.

"Can't you sell me some of that stuff?"

"Sure."

"How long would it take you to sell your stock?"

"About a week. Maybe two weeks. How it goes with me my luck."

Arthur counted twenty packages of tea. "How much a package?"

109

"Ten cents."

Then he went over the rest. Fourteen packages of coffee, at fifteen cents. Matches. Needles. Pins. Shoelaces.

"Suppose I give you twenty-five dollars and call it square?"

"No, Mister. Only what's coming to me. A price is by me a price."

"But that extra is for the time you're losing from your work when I keep you here."

"Pay for that yet—and you a friend from Adele?"

Suddenly, a worried look came into her face. "Why are you buying yourself so much tea and coffee? When will you already ever use it?"

"Oh, I have big tea parties."

"But the needles, the matches, the shoelaces. Are you maybe trying to do me a charity?"

"What nonsense! Of course not charity. But these things come in handy."

"No, Mister. Your heart is good. But *Gott sei dank,* I got yet my hands and feet to earn me my every cent."

Arthur did not say anything. He picked up a package of tea and coffee. Laid a quarter in her hand. After she had gone, he remained a long time gazing at his packages in silence.

Chapter Fourteen

Just as soon as I was well enough to go out of doors, Arthur insisted that I go driving with him in the park. It was one of those gorgeous days in autumn, trees red and gold in the sunshine, air tingling with electric freshness, Arthur Hellman at my side, his eyes solicitous upon me. This should have been the happiest day of my life. But I felt only like crying.

"I oughtn't to be playing lady, riding around with you. I ought to be back on my job."

"Oh, Adele—please. It's giving me so much pleasure. Forget your worries."

"How can I forget that Muhmenkeh spent on me all her penny-to-a-penny savings she had hoarded for her grandchild?"

"How much was it? I'll write out a check—double, triple the amount."

"I can't pay her back with your cash. I must earn the money for her as she earned it."

"Sentimental nonsense! I have lots of money. More than I need. Why shouldn't you have some of it? Call it a loan. Don't let the bitter things that happened to you make you hard. Don't refuse the right kind of help. You've gone so far. It's absurd for you to go to work in that restaurant when in six months of training you can earn a decent living."

"I don't want anything more to be grateful for."

"Gratitude! Hell! All I want is that you should have a chance to make something of yourself."

"Well, but I've got to do it in my own way. I know now that I can never fly with borrowed feathers. What I have to do is—Oh, but I feel so dumb when I try to explain this to you."

Suddenly, I became aware of Arthur's silence. His patient, trying-to-understand look exasperated me.

"You think I like living in a tenement?" I burst out. "You think I want to be a dishwasher? Like to be underpaid? But what shall I do? Take money from you? Am I not still paying for what I took from your mother?"

"Oh, Adele! Leave poor Mother out. We're both young. I understand better what you're after."

"You've been wonderful, looking me up and doing so much for me. But how can you possibly understand?"

"Why not?"

"Can a well-fed person feel what a hungry one feels? It's just that difference between you and me."

"I wonder if that's true?" Under his quiet, steady glance the simple question became almost a challenge.

I looked at his frank, kindly face. How unaware of the soul-pinching things I had known. A prince bestowing favours with a full hand. I felt so withered, so beggared beside him.

For the moment, he seemed the embodiment of the whole Hellman tribe. His ease, his smoothness, his kind good sense. Before I knew it, my feelings rushed out of me.

"The whole world is made to order for you. You've never had to go through the dirt of fighting for your life. Your ancestors did the fighting for you."

He laughed indulgently.

"You're marvellous when you're angry. Scold me some more, dear child."

"You dare ridicule me?"

"I'd dare anything—just to see you fight back. You're irresistible in revolt."

"I suffer, and you—you—"

"Oh, but you're magnificent!"

"I entertain you—do I? I amuse you? I'm to you a slumming tour. A sensation. But how absurd of me to expect you to understand."

He looked at me quietly, without speaking, the banter gone from his eyes.

"It sometimes takes all the patience and understanding that ease and education have given one to cope with the dreadful arrogance of the poor. We all have to meet life. One of the things that limits life most is each class claiming that it alone has felt and suffered. There are all kinds of struggle in the world. Poverty is one, and that you know. What difficulties I may have had in my life, you know nothing about. You limit yourself, my dear girl, when you say only the poor experience, only the poor feel and suffer."

Awed, silenced, I listened to him. All of me straining to take in more and more of this new, impassioned Arthur Hellman. But at sight of my earnest face, he stopped. The half-bantering smile came back to his eyes. He leaned forward, gave my knee a friendly little pat. "Well, really, now that you've started me, we'll have to have this out. But let's have dinner first. I think I know of a place you'd like."

It was a quiet, uncrowded tea shop on Fifth Avenue. I had

often seen the place before, but only from the outside. I remembered the latticed windows with the potted flowers standing in prim little rows. Violins. Shaded lights.

I remembered how I had watched the gay, young people laughing and talking as the grave-faced doorman bowed them in and out. How glamorous it had all seemed to me then! I hardly allowed myself even to dream how it would feel to be there with a man like Arthur Hellman.

As I followed him to a table in the far corner, I was caught up by the witchery of it all. Here was my dream before my eyes. All the polite little things those gay young men I had seen could have done for the lovely young girls, Arthur Hellman was doing for me now. He pulled out my chair. Helped me off with my coat. Noticing a draft from the open window, he rose to shut it.

How eager and alive he looked, as he moved the flowers to one side so that he could see me better across the table.

"Don't you think it's a nice cheerful old spot?"

At the sound of his voice, the magic faded. "Fine," was all I could say.

I longed to tell him right then and there how I appreciated all the little attentions with which he surrounded me. Not only what he did for me, but the way he did it. But the words wouldn't come.

Where was the Arthur Hellman of my dreams? The tall, slender god with the shining light around his head that my illusion had created? This devoted Arthur Hellman so eager to serve, to give of himself, was just a plain man.

"Why don't you smile, Adele? Why don't you look happier?"

"Well, one thing that makes me feel so wretched, you're so good to me, and I can do so little for you in return."

"Oh, Adele! How can you think about that?" He caught my

hand in his across the table. "You've done the very greatest thing in the world for me. You've made me know for the first time what it is to really care. I want to protect you, look out for you. You know you've roused something in me—you're a challenge. You know, I've just discovered that you're more than beautiful. You have—charm."

Charm! Charm! Words. Just words. Words that stopped my ears. All the inside of me was possessed by burning memories: That time at the musicale—"Don't you think you had better finish clearing the room?—You've been a fine little waitress."—The way his mother shuddered at me when I rushed to her with open arms. The way she wiped with her handkerchief the spot on her cheek I had kissed.

His ardent voice went on and on. "I had scarcely noticed you till that night. But when I saw you stand there, so little and so brave, so full of fire and so tortured—somehow, you got me then. You were romance. Personality. A personality so rich and colourful it would be joy to help in the making."

An uplifted look came into his face. His eyes suddenly far away. "I felt that the Home had hurt you. I had to follow you—save you—save you from whatever it was."

"So you followed me because you thought I had been wronged?"

His eyes held me close again.

"Have you ever seen a sensitive plant, Adele?"

"What's that?"

"It's a plant that has a myriad sensitive nerves which open to the sun. But at the first touch of a person it closes up tight and hard. Anyone who tries to force it open only breaks it. I couldn't rest until—"

"You couldn't rest until you righted the wrong that had been done to me? You *are* Sir Galahad. It's not *me* you're interested in. You're only interested in being Sir Galahad."

"That's not fair. It's not true. I may have sought you out for your sake, first. But now, I need you, Adele. I want you! I think about you all the time. What the theatre and opera would be like—with you. Listening to music with your ears. How your big eyes would open on a camping trip when you'd see for the first time the real woods, or a trout brook tumbling and singing over the rocks."

His eyes travelled over me with a glow of possession that stiffened me against him.

"I want to marry you, Adele. There's no peace for me unless you're part of my life. It's the realest thing that has ever happened to me."

Instead of triumph and elation, I felt tired. Utterly depressed.

I was hardly aware what I was saying. "Why is life like this? I was so crazy about you. I hung all my dreams around you. You are better than anything I could have imagined. But you are not the Arthur Hellman I dreamed in my heart. I want so much to go out to you. But I can't."

"I don't understand you, Adele. What are you talking about? I tell you I love you. I want to help you—and you act as though I were injuring you. Doesn't my love mean anything to you?"

He pushed his plate impatiently aside. "As I remember, you used to seem to care for me. Have you forgotten that?"

"Oh, don't—don't. I'm trying to tell you I was only in love with the idea of being in love with a man of your kind."

His eyes dropped from my face in hurt, wounded silence. When he spoke again, his voice was flat and listless: "I'm sorry. I think you're making a mistake."

116

If I could only make him understand. I liked him so much. I began desperately explaining again. "I'd never feel one of you—never one of the Hellmans. I'd never feel your equal even though I was, because I'd be smothered by your possessions. Your house, your cars, your servants, all the power that your money gives you over me. And you don't feel I'm your equal, because, even now, you're planning what you can do for me, what you can make of me. And not what I can do—what we can do together."

"My God! Adele! Stop your arrogance! Stop your neurasthenic self-analysis. I told you what you would do for me—"

"But we don't belong. You know we don't. When I sit and eat with Muhmenkeh I'm among my own. My feet on the ground of the real world I know. With you I'm walking on stilts."

A wave of red mounted to his temples. "But your world *is* mine. I've left mine. Do you actually mean all this nonsense? You actually mean you won't let me marry you when I love you? Are you sure you're not just playing a part from your romantic Russian novels? Not just dramatizing yourself as one of the persecuted—one of the Insulted and the Injured?"

I shut up completely. I only felt how good it was to have the warm security of Muhmenkeh's place to go to. I saw myself sitting with her at breakfast. A newspaper for tablecloth. Cups without handles. Poverty in all its dingy bleakness—but something—that home feeling in the heart.

In heavy silence, we drove back to Muhmenkeh. In heavy silence, we remained standing before her door. Suddenly it swept over me. It's the last time. I'm losing him. I can't let him go. . . . What do I want of him? What do I want of myself? Perhaps he was right. Perhaps I had something to give him. Why analyse? Why reason, if we love each other? My world? His? If only he

117

would sweep away with his love the doubts, the fears between us. Why didn't he do something? If only he'd unbend. Smile a little. My whole being rushed out to him this last moment. I longed to throw myself in his arms. Make him feel what was going on in me. But he stood there like a stone. Was it my pride or his pride? Something held me tight bound—shut in.

Arthur Hellman took off his hat. Bent his head a little, bowed himself out into the dark.

Chapter Fifteen

I found Muhmenkeh still waiting up for me at that late hour. "Sit yourself down, *mein kind*. Right away I'll have you a glass of tea."

The hand that set the tea before me was so gnarled, so thin. A skeleton hand with a tight-drawn skin over it. And yet that frailness had the power to keep on giving and serving.

"It joys me in my heart to see you on your feet again. Long years on you."

No questions. She simply made me feel she was standing by me no matter who this Arthur Hellman was or what my relationship to him might be.

"Tell me, Muhmenkeh," I said, brushing my cheeks against hers as she lingered beside me, "what made you take me in your home that night?"

"It gave a pull my heart to you the minute I saw you."

"Without knowing anything about me?"

"If you told me already from the beginning to the end, everything, would I maybe know you more yet? Only the heart knows. And why? Because the heart feels. And that's all we know from each other—what we feel."

"I feel you haven't always peddled with a pushcart. What was your life in Europe? Who were you before you came to America?"

Muhmenkeh's brown face broke into smiles as if each individual feature, the eyes, the lips, the cheeks smiled separately and yet together. "If I could only tell you. But it's too late now. Some other time."

Somehow I could not fall asleep that night. Stories of lonely old ghetto women I had heard about kept flying through my mind—stories that made me think of Muhmenkeh.

Maybe she was an orphan. Raised among strangers. From childhood on, a servant. Never knew home but as a servant in other people's homes. Yet from her narrow kitchen corner, she watched the lives of the people she served. They drove her—for their comfort. But what did they get out of their lives? What did they even get out of her? All they thought of her was someone to scrub and cook and clean.

In loneliness, in silence, she learned to think out her thoughts. Learned to give love, give sympathy, give understanding. Giving was really living—the only living. If you didn't give, you didn't live. Was that the secret of that something back of her eyes?

Or maybe she was the oldest of a large family. The burden-bearer of a brood of brothers and sisters. Perhaps, when she was no longer young, a young man fell in love with her. And the young man with his young eyes saw the beauty under her years. Beauty under the tired, love-starved face. Maybe his ardour, his sensitive appreciation, flung open all the shut-in doors and windows of her soul. And so, long after he had passed on, she was still growing and growing into Muhmenkeh.

Perhaps she had everything in her childhood and youth. Wealth. Family. Lovers. Friends. Maybe, after her marriage, her young husband was drafted in the Russian army. All their fortune lost in their fight to win him free. Perhaps they landed in America without a cent. Unable to find work, unable to make friends. The young man, beaten by poverty, and the new ways of the new world, fell ill and died. Maybe Muhmenkeh was too proud to tell anyone of all she had had in her rich past. But that something high-born in her was always around her like light. Peddling with her pushcart, washing dishes at the restaurant, stooping over the tub, the shine was always there.

A touch of something royal in her blood. Bowed and bent, she had grace to her—the grace that comes only to the high-born.

She had not the religiousness of the old Jewish women of the ghetto. No wig. No Sabbath candles. No praying in synagogues. But that light—don't people run to churches and synagogues looking for it? And who finds it?

The stories faded. Dreams. Pale, romantic fancies. Not the real earth from which Muhmenkeh grew.

Muhmenkeh! Oh, Muhmenkeh! Something deep in me ached to serve her. What could I do to be of some little use to her?

Then, in the stillness, in the dark, I heard my name. "Adele! Adele! Come only to me!"

It was as though some voice from another world called. Was I still dreaming? I listened. The call was repeated. Why, it was Muhmenkeh. I rushed over, turned on the gas.

"Give me your hand, Adele! Oi-i—here—" She pressed my hand over her heart. "Oi-i-i!" Her head fell back. Her hand re-laxed. My own heart began to pound in the stillness.

"Muhmenkeh! Muhmenkeh!" I cried, shaking her.

She did not answer. She did not move.

"Muhmenkeh!" I heard myself shrieking. "Muhmenkeh! Muhmenkeh! Oi-i-i-i! Muhm—men—keh! Oi-i-i-i—"

Suddenly, I realized she was dead.

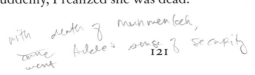

with death of muhmenkeh,
came Adele's sense of security
went

I should have called in the neighbours—tried to get help. But a strange awe held me silenced by her side. Something seemed to say itself to me out of that still face. I felt her heart beat in my heart. I felt her spirit all around me.

All night I sat in the one place, soaked in the stillness that filled the room.

Chapter Sixteen

The day after Muhmenkeh's funeral, I made a bundle of her clothes to give to Mrs. Mirsky. I went about quietly, gathering up her gray flannel petticoat, her black stockings, stiff with darns, her faded woollen dress, rubbed thin at the side where she carried her basket. Her coat, her shawl, everything went in. But when I picked up the cracked old shoes from under the bed, they seemed too much a part of Muhmenkeh for me to give up.

I put my hand into the torn lining, stained with sweat and mud. The crooked heels, worn almost to the sole. The toes split from patient trudging through endless streets, pushing up countless stairs. They were Muhmenkeh herself.

I put them back under the bed.

That night I could not sleep. I sat upon the edge of my cot, looking across at the empty bed, the empty shoes beneath it.

Loneliness pressed down on me from the four corners of the room.

Muhmenkeh—dead! That one hand of understanding life—where is it? What's to become of me now? The Hershbeins? I can't go to them. The Home? The Hellmans? I shuddered. No. Never. Enough of dishwashing. Without Muhmenkeh—that sort of thing would kill me. Back to the store? A saleslady?

Days went by. I wandered about the streets. I passed the stores.

I wanted to go in, ask for work, but my feet couldn't drag me farther than the door. And night after night more maddening grew the loneliness.

With shaking fingers, I lit the gas and began walking around. The empty shoes under the bed. Something suddenly woke up in me.

Deliberately, I put the shoes into Mrs. Mirsky's bundle. In tearing away from them, I felt that I wrenched free from the whining, wanting, sentimental old self.

I sat down on the bed to think. I saw Muhmenkeh clearer than sight. Sitting opposite me at the table. Pouring out tea from the steaming samovar. Biting the sugar, sipping from the saucer. The night before *Purim* holiday. The fun of watching her bake *mohn kuchen*. The smell of *real homemade* cake. That first melting taste after those years of loveless, tasteless food at the Home.

Purim morning. Muhmenkeh's holiday "feast of cake and wine for the little people." Mrs. Mirsky's children living next door, children from neighbouring tenements on the block, for blocks around. Little girls with baby brothers in their arms, tiny tots with dirty faces and grimy hands, unwashed necks, and tangled mops of hair that saw no comb, little roughnecks and gangsters with thievish, shifting eyes, and gentle, timid ones with their innocent wonder faces, thin, underfed, tired children, and freckled, rosy cheeks and roguish lips bursting with the joy of the street—waves of children surging around Muhmenkeh, their arms outstretched for that one little sip of wine that wasn't wine, one little bite of cake that wasn't cake. That frail, bent old thing making of her nothing a feast of plenty, feeding with it little hungry mouths that never had enough.

124

The way she stood at the centre of them, holding out her apron full of *mohn kuchens* in one hand, in the other a glass of "red wine," which she kept filling and refilling. How they smacked their lips and patted their little chests, "Yum-yum-yum! Ah-h-h! So good!"

What did it matter that the wine was but ten cents' worth of syrup bought at a pushcart diluted with sugar and water, and the *kuchen* without butter, without eggs? Muhmenkeh sent them away thrilled and filled to the brim.

All at once, I knew what I was going to do. Right here—in the heart of the tenements, where everything is so ugly and alike, this was the place to start something with Muhmenkeh's spirit in it.

I looked about the room. The sack of coffee standing in the corner, the tarnished samovar on the shelf, the huge stone fireplace crying to be used, to be warmed into life again. A landlord had built this house for himself, Muhmenkeh had told me. That was before the tenements had crowded around and shut out the light and the air. Then the place turned into a pawnshop. Later on a laundry. Muhmenkeh had found it after dozens of families had left their dirt behind them.

Muhmenkeh!

Instantly, I seized a knife and scraped the woodwork. Real walnut! But it was thick with grime and cracked with layers of old paint.

I ripped a long strip of paper off the wall. More layers of red and green ugliness. For days and days, from early morning till late at night, I kept tearing and scraping at the walls till I felt my arms would drop out of their sockets. The woodwork was worse yet. The acid paint remover ate the skin off my hands, left my fingers raw and red. The rising pile of débris and dirt seemed to suck me

125

in. I'd be just about to give up when a big chunk of paper would come off, or a bit of the real walnut would begin to show through the flaking crusts of paint. All excited again, I went at it harder than ever.

One night, completely exhausted, I sat down on a box in the middle of the floor. But with the walls almost bare, I saw how beautiful it was going to be.

The darkness of the room craved light, colour. Sunshine! I'd make it. Where were those odd pieces of Muhmenkeh's, old cheesecloth? Good enough for curtains. I dyed them bright yellow. While they were drying, I painted the walls—golden brown to blend with the walnut.

In spite of myself, it was the course of cooking and cleaning in the Training School that was the making of me. The knowledge of how to dye and paint and furnish a room—the meaning of order and cleanliness that I used to knock my head against the wall trying to learn—it was that everlasting fussiness over what I had thought nothing at all that enabled me to transform the dilapidated, three steps down from the sidewalk basement into "Muhmenkeh's Coffee Shop."

Mr. Woolworth of the Five-and-Ten-Cent Store supplied me with china, silver, and glass and the second-hand instalment man started me out with a table, a bench, and a few chairs.

On the opening night, nervously watching the door for the first customer, I went about with a rag, giving a final polish to the samovar, an extra dusting to the tables.

At last! Someone coming down the steps. With his hat over his eyes, I couldn't tell who.

"Ready for business?" he greeted, looking about the room. It was Dr. Sirowich.

"You're just in time to see me take out the *mohn kuchen*," I cried.

"That smell goes right to the spot." He sniffed like an appreciative small boy. "And you're the girl that was so sick here! Why, this is beautiful! Looks like Paris."

"I've never been in Paris."

"How did you think of it?"

"It just came to me, because I had to."

"If only Muhmenkeh could be alive to see this."

"But she is alive. I see her before my eyes, I feel her in my arms and fingers."

He gave me a look of complete understanding. "You've turned into a different person."

"I am a different person. I've lived with Muhmenkeh. I've died with her, and I'm born again."

He kept creasing the felt of his hat. Putting it down, he took my face in his hands. "I'm going right out to bring some friends back with me. They must see what you've done."

As I placed the sizzling samovar on the table, I heard them on the stairs. Suddenly, the shop boomed with the voices of men. Throwing off their hats and coats they squeezed together on the one bench and the few chairs.

Odours of tobacco, tea, and *mohn kuchen* mingled with the warm confusion of men's voices, as the cigarette stubs piled up on the bright brass trays and the smoke drifted into the dim corners of the room.

"More tea! More *kuchen!*" they kept calling.

The party ended, clicking their tall tea glasses against each other and shouting together: "Long life to Muhmenkeh's Coffee Shop! Long life to Adele, our charming hostess!"

127

Then and there they organized themselves charter members of my enterprise and vowed to become "pullers-in" for the coming season.

Dr. Sirowich took down his coat. But he only put his arm into one sleeve. He sat back, his gaze wandering about the room. The others lingered, then sat down again with their coats over their knees, their hats in their hands. At last, Dr. Sirowich pulled out his wallet. "Well, tell us the bad news. What's the check?"

"Check?" I flushed with embarrassment. "To my charter members? Charge money for the pleasure of watching you eat my cake and drink my tea?"

"A fine business woman you'll make," Dr. Sirowich scolded. His eyes searched the room until they lighted on the brass bowl under the samovar. He took it in his hand ceremoniously. With an expression of earnest concentration, he counted aloud, "Four glasses of tea, forty cents. Two helpings of *kuchen,* thirty cents."

He dropped the coins slowly, clinking them for good luck. He passed the bowl around. The clinking resounded again, as one after another paid his bill.

Under the inspiration of that friendliness, the brass bowl became my cashier and cash register all in one. On the table by the door it stood. And all who came, strangers or friends, fell into the spirit of this informal way of paying. They dropped the correct coins into the bowl, or, if need be, made change from its trusting contents.

Every night I eagerly counted my cash bowl. From day to day I worked. To-morrow's menu depended on what I took in today. A full cash bowl after lunch—more dishes for dinner.

"Will you have *gefülte* fish?"

A glance at the cash bowl. "To-morrow will be *gefülte* fish."

"I'd like to bring some girls from uptown for dinner. Can you make chicken salad?"

"Why, of course, chicken salad," feeling sure the butcher would trust me.

Excitement kept me going. Four o'clock in the morning—up and out to the market. The butcher, the baker, the pushcart peddlers knew me.

"Hey! Red-Head! Here's a bargain for you! Only six cents a pound."

"I can buy apples two pounds for a nickel."

"Not goods like mine. Give only a bite. Wine from heaven it tastes."

"Two pounds nine cents?"

"Oi-i weh! Have a heart! I also got to live! Only for you—a nickel a pound." He started to weigh them.

"Take off those rotten apples."

"Rotten? A little speck only on the side from where it touched itself by the barrel."

"Put on another or I won't buy. Take your hand off the scale. I'm paying for apples."

Once I had hated the sordid sight of women fighting at the pushcarts to get the food a penny cheaper for their families. Now bargaining became a game with a new meaning for me. Giving my people the most for the least money was my way of working out the hungers I had suffered.

Morning after morning, I'd return from the market staggering with my load of supplies.

Every day something happened in the shop to draw me out of myself. What stories my open cash bowl held!

Those two well-fed, well-dressed college boys. They thought it a great joke to eat as much as they could and sneak out without paying. I let them do it once. The second day, I stopped them just as they were about to slip out. "Are you too poor to pay?" I asked.

They never showed up again.

The poor shop girls—they always wanted an extra dessert and couldn't afford to pay for it. What did it matter if one here and there didn't pay it all? The good customers made it possible for me to smile away an occasional loss.

How some of them did eat!

It was a sight to watch Mrs. Goldstein, the dressmaker, giving her children their daily dinner. Her red, swollen eyes lighted as she filled Gertie's and Becky's trays with food. But when I passed her table she furtively covered a dish on her full tray. I deliberately turned my back when I saw the uneasy look on her face as she dropped the money in the bowl.

Night after night, Mrs. Goldstein put a little more on each child's tray. Night after night, the coins she dropped in the bowl grew smaller and the vehemence with which she stuffed her pair grew louder.

"Gertie! Eat! Eat, I tell you!"

"Becky! A thunder should strike you! Mamma says eat!"

After the fourth or fifth course poor Becky and Gertie couldn't force down all their eager mother kept piling on them. They were just picking and pecking and spoiling one new dish after another. And that I couldn't stand.

Following her outside, I spoke to her: "Mrs. Goldstein! Are you sure you and Gertie and Becky ate only twenty-five cents' worth to-night?"

"What a question yet!" she flared, shoving the children out ahead of her.

That was the end of the Goldsteins. For a long time, I couldn't rid myself of the persistent sense of guilt. to feel guilty for what?

Cheap food that wasn't scrimped and cheated and the friendly atmosphere drew people from all parts of the city. The very people I most wanted to meet became my daily customers. Little by little, my basement kitchen turned into an artist's corner.

Joseph Berman's pictures on the wall struck the first spark. One day, he came up to me shyly with some canvases under his arm.

"I have no place to show my stuff. The galleries uptown don't know that I exist. You have so much space on your walls, and so many come here. Perhaps you would let me put up a few?"

Spoil the bare beauty of my place with those hodge-podge paintings of his! I had worked too hard for this precious plainness to ruin it with crazy pictures that made no sense to me.

"Drive nails into my lovely painted walls?" I tried to laugh him off.

"I'll put up a moulding. I'll hang them from the top. I'll do anything—only for a chance to show my work."

A chance to show his work! His eagerness, I understood that. I let him have an entire wall.

What a joke it was on me when the critics hailed him as a great event in new art. They came trailing into my shop at all hours to see his work.

One exhibit led to another. The walls became a constantly changing gallery for new art.

Meeting new people! New people! The one thing I longed for and dreamed of when I strained to reach the Hellmans now came to my very door.

I went out to sweep away the snow from my shop. I stum-

Arthur a musician
Adele a Joseph

131

bled over someone hunched on the top step. Startled, the broom dropped from my hand.

The man lurched forward, half drunk, trying to help me pick it up.

It was snowing hard, and he had no overcoat. His face was so comically puckered with the cold, the next thing I knew, I asked him to come in, have dinner.

Warmed by the food, he began to talk. "So you're a cook, Red-Head. This is your job, is it?"

"And what's yours?"

"A poet," he said. Which seemed unbelievable enough. He was bald. Small eyes sunk in a fat face. The last person in the world to look like the ideal face of Shelley or Byron.

He sat around after his meal scribbling on the back of the menu card. All of a sudden, he noisily cleared his throat, clapped his hands for silence. I was in a panic. I couldn't have my people imposed upon by this drunken man, even though he imagined himself a poet.

There he was on his feet, swaying slightly as he held on to the table. Out he launched in a rollicking tone. The gayest sort of a ballad of Muhmenkeh's Coffee Shop.

His fat face beamed at the applause.

Eager young people flocked to his table, reciting and chanting and discussing for hours. I thought they'd never stop and go home. That was the beginning of our poetry evenings around the fireplace.

The day I paid my first instalment for a second-hand piano, everybody rejoiced with me. They left their suppers to exult over it and help the truckman squeeze it through the narrow door.

Someone started to play. Then another and another. The room filled with the music for which I was starving—Chopin, Beethoven, Brahms, Moussorgsky, and then Chasin's *Procession* which Rachmansky had played. With the beauty it brought, came the pain and the longing and the terrible unrest.

Chapter Seventeen

My eyes wandered over the room, rested on a young couple who came for their dinner every Wednesday. I used to await their coming with a loving jealousy, an aching gladness that all my absorption in my work could not shut out.

When they came in, they seemed not to touch the earth. Young gods flying triumphant over the rest of the world. Untouched by the hurts and needs that ate into the lives of others. Safe and sure in each other.

Smiles met them from all the tables. Buzzes of conversation were left in their wake. They seemed almost unreal in their perfect happiness.

The frequenters of Muhmenkeh's Coffee Shop never tired discussing their romantic story. Six years married, and still falling more and more in love.

They had met as students in medical college. Penniless when they married. The instalment man set them up, their doctor's office. Now they were among the busiest, the most successful physicians on the East Side.

My hand would go out to her as she went by. An electric happiness seemed to pass through my fingers right to my heart.

It was good to look at them, leaning toward each other, as if they had just met after ages of separation.

I sat watching them—fascinated—trying to imagine how it must feel to be regarded with such worship. Was she so loved because her eyes were so beautiful or were her eyes so beautiful because she was so loved?

It was hot and stuffy that night. She made a motion to push back the scarf she wore. With the quick eagerness of the lover, he was at her side, his hand gently smoothing her shoulder as he removed the scarf.

How beautiful was that tender gesture! It made everything around unimportant. Quite suddenly, I felt a little ache in my heart.

All at once I saw that the happy young people were moving in couples. Why had I not noticed this before?

I felt overwhelmingly alone.

Lonelier and lonelier, as one after another finished their dinner and hurried out.

The place grew terribly big and empty.

I started to close the windows, bolt the back door. High beyond reach was the centre chandelier. As usual, I climbed on the chair to turn it out. Again I saw the young doctor's eyes as he looked at her. He would have turned out the light for her. His arm would have come down with that special, intimate touch with which he caressed her shoulder as he removed her scarf.

The Coffee Shop—the work—the people—it was a great adventure. But not enough to fill my life. I was young. I wanted love as much as all those other young people.

Muhmenkeh would have been gladdened by their happiness, I told myself. But I'm not Muhmenkeh. I'm not gladdened by their joy. I'm only envious.

It was long past closing time. I sat there too tired to turn out the other lights.

Someone came in. I wasn't going to wait on anyone more that night. I wouldn't even look up.

The man rapped the table to call my attention. But I sat on, inert. As the rap was repeated, I pulled myself up, my mouth open to say, "Too late! The place is closed!" when my eyes fell on his face. It was Jean Rachmansky. He—of all people! What was he doing here—at this hour?

"A pot of coffee and cigarettes," he mumbled.

"What kind of cigarettes?"

"Any kind."

I stood staring at him. What had happened? How came he to this neighbourhood?

Unshaven. Unkempt. Lost-looking. His tie slewed around under his left ear. His eyes staring unseeingly out of their dark sockets as if he hadn't slept in a year.

As he drank his coffee and smoked his cigarettes, I saw his gaze wander over to the piano.

I was wide awake now. Surprised. Excited. I wanted awfully to sit down at his table and talk to him. But I saw there was something weighing on his mind. It was like a wall around him that I did not dare break through.

Only after he had walked out and it was too late, I felt the courage come to me to ask him the thousand questions that were on my tongue.

Every night, after that, I kept hoping he might drop in again. But no further sign of him.

When I went to the market, I found myself searching the faces of the passers-by, wondering if he were anywhere in the neighbourhood.

I had almost given up hoping to see him when, one evening, late again, he walked in.

Again he ordered coffee and cigarettes in that abstracted way of his—without looking up. Again his eyes went straight to the piano. He jumped from his chair in a quick, nervous manner. Looked anxiously around. Seeing he was alone, he stole over and began to play. By the time I had brought him his coffee, he had forgotten what he had ordered.

Stray chords. Whispering passages and then again that *Procession*. From under the earth—the dumb, the voiceless seemed to stir and breathe. Everything that longed for sun and had no sun, the hungry, the homeless, echoed and mingled in the music that sobbed under his fingers.

Like a soul shooting out of its dark body, so a new melody leaped up from the groaning, the travail of those earthy chords. Luminous, free, it floated into space until it merged with sun and cloud and stars.

In the flashing reality of that vision, I caught a glimpse of my real self—the real selves of the millions defrauded, defeated, blocked from the life that was meant to be theirs. It was theirs—if only they could see. anything possible -- have to get it

If only they could hear such music.

Muhmenkeh's eyes had never been clouded by fear. Her real self had walked the streets every day. Bent over the washtub, the steaming sink, or counting out pennies into dirty hands, she had lived as if she had always heard such harmonies.

He stopped. But the air around him was still full of his music.

"You? You here?" Surprise and recognition came in to his face. "And I've been here before and didn't recognize you. I've heard of you and this place. I wanted to see you, ever since that concert at Arthur Hellman's, but somehow I've been doing nothing but drift."

He kept staring at me. "The same eyes. The same face. That time, all those people around me, smiling, flattering. But not knowing it. Not getting it. One little living point. Your face. You understood it then. You understand now."

"But I don't understand. I only feel it. That's why it hurts so!"

"No. It hurts because you understand."

"You mean I've lived it?"

"Yes. Arthur Hellman told me about you—when you spoke at some meeting once. He came back after that so excited and worried. He described you to me—how you burst into flame—then vanished. I thought of you when I, too, broke away."

"You left Arthur Hellman?"

He got up from the piano stool, lit a cigarette, stood tilting back a chair, looking at me. A whole map of struggle was in the lines of his dark face. The shadows under his eyes were battlefields where feelings and ideas fought their way into rhythm and sound more real than life. And yet it was a young face.

"Yes." He sat down wearily at the table, leaned his head in his hands. "I walked out."

"Walked out—? Tell me."

He only looked at me. I felt the weariness that crushed what he wanted to say.

As quietly as I could I took back the coffee thinned with the melting ice, brought back another glass, fresh ice, and some of my *mohn kuchen.*

He ate and drank. "But this is Poland, this *kuchen.*" He smiled as he looked about the room. "This place feels European. It makes me think of the *krechma* where my father used to play."

"Tell me, how did you come to Arthur Hellman? Why did you leave him?"

"Why did I leave him? Sometimes I wonder myself. Such a fine man! Just because of his fineness, I let him lead me too far. He would have made me. But he would have made me a performer. I must compose."

"Couldn't you do both?"

"I thought at first I could. Arthur told me I could. But to be a protégé you have to be a social creature. You must dilly-dally at teas. Play pretty pieces for the ladies. It eats up your time. Worse— it eats up what's in you. So much buzzing about me. Arthur, with all good intention for my welfare, kept bringing his friends to meet me at all hours of the day. I wanted quiet, solitude for work. I couldn't get it."

"And so you left?"

"I walked out. I had to. How I fought against myself when I saw them going on with the publicity for my début. And then—"

"And then?"

"A week before the big concert, I walked out."

He began pacing the room restlessly. "I blame myself bitterly. If I was weak enough to be drawn into it—I should have had strength enough to go through with it. Arthur was always so patient, so anxious to understand. Yet I did that to him."

"We've both been wicked, cruel to the Hellmans."

I thought of that hurt look in Mrs. Hellman's face the day I broke loose. I wondered how Arthur had looked when he found Rachmansky gone?

"Why do we hurt people so? Is it because we're such ingrates?"

"They gave us what they thought we ought to have. But we wanted something that no individual could give. Something that we ourselves must wrest from life. The amazing thing to me is that we expected so much from them and were hurt because it wasn't humanly possible for them to live up to our expectations. Just because they were kind to us, we demanded friendship, love, understanding, the very things they, with all their wealth, lacked."

"Some day I hope to have the courage to speak up at another public meeting of the Home. Tell them out of a full heart how I'm really indebted to them for the richest, deepest stimulus of my life. The very inferiority which their kindness burned into me drove me to get on my own feet in the quickest possible way."

We both laughed at the absurdity of such an anticlimax.

"Our punishment is that we'll never have another chance to explain ourselves to them and to remember always how profoundly they have helped us—not only to find ourselves.—Through them, we found each other."

I looked again into the eyes that hadn't slept for a year. The battlefield of thought and feeling brooding in that dark face.

"Where are you living now?"

"Oh—I? . . . Well, just at present, I'm at the Bowery Lodging House. To be exact, corner Grand Street and Bowery."

I saw a swift picture of him leaving Hellman's beautiful Washington Mews studio. Leaving the quiet, the peace of the aristocratic street for the noisy, crowded streets of the poor. Shoved about in the jam of market baskets and pushcarts, deafened by the clamour of haggling and bargaining and the cries of the children. On and on—not knowing where. Weary with the confusion of himself, falling in line with the homeless ones who pay fifteen cents a night to stretch out their bones in darkness, in dirt. But there was something in Rachmansky's face that pushed aside the insult of pity.

In the most natural way, he began to tell me all about himself before he met Arthur Hellman. He had come from Warsaw, Poland. There he had earned his living as a piano teacher, devoting all his spare time to writing music. His Sundays, his holidays, his rest and his sleep, his longing to know people, to make friends—everything went into his passion for music.

"I had once seen a picture of the Resurrection by Signorelli," he went on. "In this painting the people are shown struggling up out of the black earth—a foot, a hand, a whole figure. I wanted to express in music that struggle up out of the earth. The urge to break through the earthy things that hold us down. . . .

"I had just begun my composition when the war broke out. I was drafted. All music stopped in me. After the release—I fled to America. On the boat, the silence, the sea, the sky. Suddenly, the whole vision of the Resurrection burst upon me. . . .

"A piano! I had to have a piano. There was no piano in the steerage. I knew there was one up above, on the first-class deck. My whole body and soul craved through my fingers for release—release. I was like a sleepwalker who stops at nothing. When I got to the barred door, I found a space at the bottom of the grating to squeeze through. I managed to get to the second-class deck. And again I found my way through another barred door. I don't know how, but I did it. The touch of those keys to my fingers was like water in a wilderness. I began to play. Arthur found me. The rest you know."

We were quiet, voiceless. Silence like a hidden bond of communication between us.

"Isn't it strange," he mused, unconsciously tracing my initials

141

with his finger dipped in the spilled coffee. "I haven't found any-one to whom to talk as I talk to you in all these years I've been in this country. And I know nothing about you except—except—" He just looked at me and smiled.

As naturally as he told me about himself, I found myself telling him things in my life I thought I had forgotten. Father's love of music. The operas and concerts he took me to when I was barely able to walk. The way he would explain to me what each piece meant, as though I were a grown-up. When he fell ill, he told us to pawn his lodge insurance to get a second-hand phonograph. His last dying days. The phonograph going all the time. Between rack-ing coughs, his favourite pieces—*Pagliacci*—*Ave Maria*—Masse-net's *Elegy*.

Then I told him of Muhmenkeh. How she had spent on me in my illness the money she had saved to bring her grandchild to America. Muhmenkeh's death.

"I haven't seen that picture that you speak of that has so in-spired you. But that night of terror, after Muhmenkeh's funeral, I was like those people bound to the earth, struggling with their hands and feet to tear themselves out of the earth. That night when, in the midst of my terrible loneliness, I suddenly stopped whining like an alley cat and began working out my vision of Muhmenkeh's Coffee Shop, I felt what you felt when the music of the Resurrection burst upon you."

"If only the Hellmans knew how much we are indebted to them," he said, "they who consciously tried to do so much for us that didn't turn out right—should accidentally have done the deep-est thing of all—brought us together. How grateful we are, after all. If only we could make them feel that their well-meant blunder-ing efforts to help have gone deeper than their plans. I went back to Arthur a few days after I left. He was fine. He said he understood. But after all—" He shrugged.

"We can't undo the hurt to them. But—"

Somehow the air grew too thick for conversation. An excitement and a calm filled my soul as I looked at him. He was as much home as Muhmenkeh. But more.

Was it the night, or the excitement of our confession, or just the youth of us? Suddenly, as we faced each other across the table, he pushed back his chair. "Can't we go up on the roof where we can breathe?"

I hurried ahead of him, up the dark stairs, fearful lest our hands might touch. As I had felt myself drawn in by his music, so I now felt his eyes, his lips, the charm about his very breath, drawing me in, conquering me.

It was still dark on the roof. But we could feel the light behind the sky ready to break through. Mounds of huddled humans showed where families had come to sleep in the air.

The intense quiet. The stars in their silence shining over us.

We stood fascinated by the people so close together in their sleep.

A baby's cry. The mother drew it to her breast and fed it.

One moment of panic, as we felt each other, saw each other, without looking. One breathless moment—his hand closed over mine.

Suddenly, the people about us, the sky, the stars were blotted out. Nothing existed but us.

With one impulse we turned to seek once more the solitude below. As the door of my room closed behind us that which we fought and feared swept us together.

Chapter Eighteen

Not since Muhmenkeh's Coffee Shop had been in existence was there such a crowd as on the evening Jean Rachmansky played. Everybody on the block wanted to get in. What a hurdy-gurdy of life-starved faces! Students, plumbers, salesmen, tailors. Slim stenographers and school teachers side by side with shawled *yentehs* and gray-bearded old men.

As I stood at the doorway, trying to hold back the jam of people fighting to get in, I thought of the uptown audience that Arthur Hellman had invited to hear Jean. Those patrons of genius, sitting back in proper poses of attention—and this rapacious mob, mad for music, pushing greedily for places nearer the piano.

"Oi-i! What a player!"

"He knows how—that feller!"

"Who is he? From where comes he?" they nudged one another.

"Sh-h-h! Still! sh-h!"

Jean turned the piano into a human voice, waking them out of sodden sleep. Just listening was living. Life filtered through tired bodies, bent backs. Heads lifted. Fear and worry fled from their eyes. For an instant, they breathed in a fullness of life denied them in life.

Again and again he played, and they kept clamouring for

more. Ancient Hebrew melodies, folk tunes, chords that struck at the very roots of their long-forgotten past. Weeping at a funeral, dancing at a wedding.

The last notes of an old lullaby died away. The silence still vibrated with the memories of homeland—far away—forever beyond reach. Their eyes fixed—lost in a maze of melody.

Then they broke loose and stormed around him.

Women kissed his sleeve. Others seized his hand, pressed their withered cheeks against it.

"Long life on you! Golden heart!"

"Blessed should be your every little finger!"

"I got a boy seven years old. Oi-i! Tell me only—how can he grow up for a player like you?"

Everybody talked to him at the same time. Everybody had to be heard first.

"I would like my Minnie should learn from you. When should I maybe send her yet? When?"

"Young man! Mister! Your playing—ay—yay—velvet and silk!"

The news of Jean's playing spread. All kinds of people flocked to him, begging him to teach them.

"I'm a cloaks and suits salesman, but I'm crazy to learn music on the side." It was a young man with a shrewd business face. Hungry, restless eyes, wide with childlike innocence.

Jean glanced at his stubby hand.

"I've tried taking up painting. But that sort of thing is too slow for me. I'm a salesman. I got to move quick. It takes so long to finish a picture. But music—that's different. I know I can get the go of it quick."

Jean turned from the salesman only to face a more embarrassing plea of Mrs. Ginsberg, the landlady, that he teach her son Danny.

The day before he had given the boy a hearing. "Why force music on the poor child?" he told her again.

"But I'll pay you more than plenty, only to learn him. I want to buy me the pleasure to show off my Danny for company."

Jean shifted about uncomfortably, walked over to the window, looked out. "You see, I have so little time—"

"No time for my Danny?" she flared. "My Danny ain't good enough for you to learn him? The janitor's boy a nothing, a nobody—him you take on—for him you get time? What?" She seized her son by the hand and swept out.

At the door she was met by another mother with her boy.

"*Nu? Nu?* Did he take on your Danny."

"Ach! the *Schnorrer!* I wouldn't let my Danny learn from such a *Kabtzin.* All musicians are beggars. Never got enough for rent. Let my son better have a head for business and he'll buy up pianos and piano-players like him."

Jean remained standing at the window, a sad smile of utter helplessness on his face. A girl appeared in the doorway, hesitated a moment, then crossed over.

"Mr. Rachmansky!" She touched his sleeve, paused for breath, then raced on impetuously: "I heard you play. I couldn't speak to you when the crowd was around you, but now, I can't help myself. I had to come. I don't know what I'm saying—that's why I'm so bold. I must beg of you something. Don't refuse me!"

It was Mashah Mendel, the "piano teacher" of the block. A face scarred and weather-beaten with struggle, but the untamed gleam still in her eyes.

"I never had a chance to learn music. I picked it up for myself here and there. What little I know I teach. I studied stenography and typewriting, but I hated it so, and once, while out of a job, despair drove me to plunge into the thing I loved to do. I charge only twenty-five cents a lesson, two lessons for forty-five cents. Because I'm cheap and they can bargain me down a nickel on two lessons, they come to me. You see, I earn so little, I never had the money for good teachers. I came to ask you to give me a hearing."

Rachmansky walked over to the piano. "Come, sit down. Play a C major scale."

Mashah Mindel sat down full of scornful confidence.

"A scale you want—what?"

He watched her struggling fingers a moment.

"Oh—n-n-no!" He shook his head, then bent over her. "Look, this way."

"Ah-h!" she cried. "Your notes! They sing! They live!"

She tried again, but self-consciousness overcame her. Her hands dropped.

"God! Will I ever in a million years play like you? But now I'll never have rest till I can do it. Oh, that music—that singing tone that you have! My God! If you would only teach me!"

He looked at the stiff hands, at the middle-aged face. "How old are you?"

"What's age when you love a thing as I love music?"

"But it's impossible to develop technique at your age."

"How do you know what my will may not achieve at my age? Socrates was just my age when he began to learn how to read and write, and yet he made of himself one of the world's greatest thinkers."

"Thinking is different from playing the piano. You think with

147

your mind. To play you must have supple fingers. Your hands are your tools."

"Have you read the *Life of Helen Keller?* Deaf and dumb and blind—and yet can those who have the tools of sight and hearing and speech give the world the thoughts she has given?"

Seeing him susceptible to her insistent demands, she stormed on:

"People like you are just as heartless to a beginner as the rich to the poor. I have nothing in my life but this music for which you say I'm too old, but I won't give it up—I can't give it up."

"Hear good music. Make that satisfy you."

She whirled about, pointing an accusing finger at him.

"You're like the rich man sitting back at a feast telling the beggar: 'Still your hunger watching me eat.' You think music is only for such as you who have genius? I, too, want music. I love it. And the children who come to me love it. For their sake—I beg you—help me!"

After she had gone, Jean turned to me. "A piano-mover has to have a license to move pianos, but any stenographer out of a job can hang out a sign, 'piano teacher.' With her stiff fingers she can never learn to play. And yet—how do I know what will may not achieve? How could anyone turn down those eyes?"

A silence fell upon us. Mashah Mendel's outburst suddenly made me realize that the chasm of genius was as real as the chasm of wealth that would have separated me from Arthur Hellman. And yet, why did I feel closer to Rachmansky than to Shlomoh Hershbein, who was a plain plodder like me?

"How is it that I'm not frightened by your genius, Jean? How could I feel so at home with a man who belongs so much to the world as you?"

"My genius—whatever that is—is dead without you."

He drew my hand against his.

"You brought me back to life—our own people. There's an atmosphere here." His eyes turned from me to look about the shop and then back to me again.

He laughed, his eye holding me. "Is it you or this place of yours? Why, since that night—

"I've done more real work than in all the sterile months and years in that stifling studio.

"Adele!" he cried, crushing me to him. "Can't you feel how I need you? How we need each other?"

Chapter Nineteen

Jean looked down from the top rung of the ladder through tangled Swiss curtains. "There! Have I made it even?"

"Yes. But you don't hang curtains as well as you play the piano. I let you help me this time only—in honour of our great guest."

"Will our little immigrant appreciate the preparations we're making for her arrival?" He laughed, looking down at me.

"Muhmenkeh did not stop to ask if I'd appreciate what she did for me."

He came down the ladder and stood watching me arrange the flowers in front of the brass-framed picture of Muhmenkeh's grandchild.

Even before we married, we sent passage money for Shenah Gittel to come to America, as Muhmenkeh had planned to do. When we leased our flat above the Coffee Shop, the room for Shenah Gittel was our first thought.

The quaint little face brought back to me Muhmenkeh's face when she first showed me the picture. "Ai-ai-ai! Is she yet beautiful? Long years on her! God should only let me live long enough to see her here in good luck."

"Shenah Gittel!" I said softly, taking the picture in my hands.

"Muhmenkeh saved me once when I was so lost and unhappy. Now she's saving us in our happiness."

I clasped the hand Jean held over my shoulder. "This child will be our hostage to fortune—keep us from forgetting the rest of the world in each other."

Jean took the picture out of my hand. "H'm! Not too good looking. Dumpy little body. Big, thick nose."

"Well, Muhmenkeh had such a big, thick nose."

He put down the picture and searched my face. "And you're pretty plain yourself. Except for your eyes, your hair, and a few other little things."

His gaze lingered caressingly. For a moment, there was no consciousness for us but each other's eyes.

"I never knew that joy could be deeper than sorrow. And yet, why do we fear it so?"

He brushed the back of his hand against my cheek. "Do you fear it?" he asked.

"Yes. I fear. This lull of peace—a mere breath may blow it away."

"I know. We're still like lost sheep. We've been so many ages without shelter, we can't believe we've found home."

Together, we went downstairs to the Coffee Shop for breakfast.

As I passed him his cup, my hand shook so, some of the coffee spilt into the saucer.

"You're as excited as if you yourself were coming to America."

"Why shouldn't I be excited? Muhmenkeh's grandchild—coming to us."

"You funny little philanthropist! You're walking nobly in the footsteps of Mrs. Hellman."

"Of course I am. Poor Mrs. Hellman! She felt guilty for her wealth, and I feel guilty for being so happy."

"And I ought to feel guilty for taking so much from you. But I don't. I love to be indebted to you." He picked up a piece of toast. "You're twice the staff of my life. Perhaps I lean too much on you. Perhaps you're making things too easy for me."

I touched the old lines on the young forehead. "Things easy for you!—Oh, my dearest!"

Swiftly he was out of his chair, standing beside me. He drew my head against him, his musician's fingers through my hair. God held us in His Arms as we rested against each other.

"One thing I promise you," I said, at last. "If by any chance we lose each other, I'll never forget this. It'll be a rock under my feet, the mere memory that we've had each other."

"Don't talk of loss." His voice was like a cry. "I couldn't endure the old loneliness. Even my work, with all the passionate effort I put into it—it could only struggle up twisted and unflowering through that barren cold. Now my music bursts into blossom through the warmth of you."

All the way to the boat, our hands did not even touch. We walked the streets, sat in the car, like ordinary people. But our hearts sang with the oneness of us two.

As we stood there on the gangplank before the eager boatload searching the wharf for friends, all at once a million fears seized me at the responsibility we had undertaken.

"How can we, being only what we are, live up to the demands Shenah Gittel will make on us? What didn't I expect from Mrs. Hellman—"

"You little goose! Of course we can't live up to all Shenah

Gittel will expect. We can only give her the chance to get it for herself."

to what Adele was asking for

Jean's grip tightened on my arm. Suddenly, out of the many faces, we saw Muhmenkeh's face—Muhmenkeh's grandchild coming toward us.

The End

About the Author

Anzia Yezierska (1880?–1970) is the author of many books including *Bread Givers* and *Salome of the Tenements*.

About the Editor

Katherine Stubbs is a Ph.D. Candidate in the Department of English at Duke University.

Library of Congress Cataloging-in-Publication Data

Yezierska, Anzia, 1880?–1970.

Arrogant Beggar / by Anzia Yezierska; introduction by

Katherine Stubbs

p.   cm.

ISBN 0-8223-1752-4 (cl : alk. paper) —

ISBN 0-8223-1749-4 (pa : alk. paper)

1. Jewish women—New York (N.Y.)—Fiction.

2. Women immigrants—New York (N.Y.)—Fiction.   3. Working class

women—New York (N.Y.)—Fiction.   4. Boardinghouses—New York

(N.Y.)—Fiction.   I. Title.

PS3547.E95A89   1996

813'.52—dc20   95-39037   CIP